The Weight

ALSO IN LEGEND BY ALLEN STEELE

Orbital Decay
Clarke County, Space
Lunar Descent
Labyrinth of Night
Rude Astronauts

THE WEIGHT

Allen Steele

LEGEND

First published in the United Kingdom in 1995 by
Legend Books
Random House UK Limited
20 Vauxhall Bridge Road, London, SW1V 2SA

Random House Australia (Pty) Limited
20 Alfred Street, Milsons Point, Sydney, NSW 2061
Australia

Random House New Zealand Limited
18 Poland Road, Glenfield, Auckland 10,
New Zealand

Random House South Africa (Pty) Limited
PO Box 337, Bergvlei, South Africa

Random House UK Limited Reg. No. 954009

ISBN: 0 09 948901 5

Typeset by Deltatype Ltd, Ellesmere Port, S. Wirral
Printed in England by Clays Ltd, St Ives plc

For Bob Liddil and Terry and Linda Kepner . . .
the portable gang.

Acknowledgement

During the creation of this short novel, I researched a number of subjects, ranging from Jupiter and its moons to artificial intelligence to Mormon history and ethics; none was more daunting, however, than post-polio syndrome. In this instance I was blessed with the expert advice of Samanda b Jeude and her organization, Electrical Eggs.

Electrical Eggs is a group of science fiction fans who provide access services at SF conventions for disabled persons. If you wish to know more about the Eggs, please send a self-addressed, stamped envelope to: Electrical Eggs, Ltd., Post Office Box 308, Lebanon, GA. 30146 USA.

September 1991–June 1992
St Louis, Missouri,
Smithville, Tennessee

Leaving the Moon

THE FIRST TIME I saw the DSV *Medici Explorer* was during primary approach by the lunar shuttle which ferried me to its parking orbit six hundred kilometres above the Moon. As the spider-like shuttle coasted around the sunlit limb of the eastern terminator and passed above the dark expanse of Mare Crisium, a small artificial constellation gently hove into view above the silver-grey horizon, gradually growing larger as the klicks fell away. The *Medici Explorer* and the three drone freighters that it shepherds slowly swelled in size, gaining dimension and detail with each passing minute, until the vessel could be seen in all its enormous complexity.

The *Medici Explorer* is fifty-six metres in length, from the gunmetal-grey nozzle of its primary engine to the grove of antennae and telescopes mounted on its barrel-shaped hub module; at the tips of its three arms – which were not yet rotating – the spacecraft is about forty-six metres in diameter. Pale blue moonlight reflected dully from the tube-shaped hydrogen, oxygen and water tanks clustered in tandem rows between the hub and the broad, round radiation shield at the stern. Extended on a slender boom aft of the shield, behind the three gimbal-mounted manoeuvring engines, is the gas-core nuclear engine, held at safe distance from the crew compartments at the forward end of the vessel. Although the reactor stack in Arm Three is much closer to the hub, it is heavily shielded and cannot harm the crew when it is in operation.

The *Medici Explorer* was already awake and thriving. Two days earlier, it had departed from Armstrong Station, the lunar-orbit spacedock where it had been docked since the completion of its last voyage six months ago. During the interim, while its crew rested at Descartes City and the precious cargo of Jovian helium-3 was unloaded from the freighters and transported to Earth, the *Medici*

Explorer had undergone the routine repairs necessary before it could make its next trip to Jupiter. Now, at long last, the giant spacecraft had been towed by tugs to a higher orbit where it was reunited with its convoy.

The shuttle made its final approach toward the vessel's primary docking collar on the hub module. On the opposite side of the docking collar, anchored to a truss which runs through a narrow bay between the outboard tanks, was the *Marius*, a smaller spacecraft used for landings. The fact that the ship's boat was docked with the larger vessel was evidence that the *Medici Explorer*'s crew had returned from shore leave; more proof could be seen from the lights which glowed from the square windows of Arm One and Arm Two.

Red and blue navigational beacons arrayed along the super-structure illuminated more details: an open service panel on the hub where a robot was making last-minute repairs; a hardsuited space worker checking for micrometeorite damage to the hull; the round emblem of Consolidated Space Industries, the consortium which owns the vessel, painted on the side of the hub. Then the shuttle slowly yawed starboard, exposing its airlock hatch to the docking collar, and the *Medici Explorer* drifted away from its windows.

During the last few minutes of the flight, I got one brief, final look at home. Earth was a mosaic of blues and whites and greens and tans, as gloriously alive as the Moon is sterile. There was just enough time for me to have irrevocable regrets about the long journey ahead before there was the hard thump of docking.

The shuttle pilot, a young woman with crewcut blond hair and a perpetual scowl on her sunburned face, ran her hands across the myriad toggles and buttons on her dashboard. A faint hiss as atmospheric pressure equalized between the airlocks, then an annunciator buzzed, signalling that the hatch was ready to be opened. She didn't bother to unbuckle her harness; she would be here only as long as it took for her to unload her sole passenger.

'OK, you're here,' she said, cocking her thumb toward the airlock hatch behind her. 'Out that way and through the tunnel. Watch your head and don't forget your stuff.'

'Thanks,' I said, unsnapping the harness and carefully pushing my way out of my seat. 'See you when I get back.'

It was meant as a polite goodbye. I had heard the same thing said many times, from one spacer to another, during the last several Earthdays I had spent on the Moon, waiting for my assignment to begin, but for some reason she found obscure humour in the statement.

She laughed out loud, not very pleasantly. 'I won't count on it if you don't,' she replied, looking over her shoulder at me, and I recognized that as yet another customary exchange among spacers. Its meaning was all too clear: nobody lives forever . . . .

Not an encouraging thought. But then again, Jupiter is a most dangerous destination.

The first crewman I met upon clambering through the shuttle's short access tunnel into the *Medici Explorer*'s airlock was William Smith-Tate, the ship's chief engineer. Had I been clairvoyant and known what he and I would go through in the months ahead, I would have ducked straight back through the airlock and into the shuttle.

Bill was a squat, big-chested, broad-shouldered man whose dense beard and wide forehead gave him a brooding appearance, and he didn't seem particularly inclined to welcome me aboard his ship. His handshake was firm, his calloused palm almost completely enveloping mine, and it was hard not to wince at his grasp.

'You're the last one aboard,' he said gruffly, almost an admonishment; only later did I realize that he had a thousand other things to worry about during the last two hours before launch, and the late arrival of a passenger was far down on his list of priorities. 'I'll have my boy take you to your quarters . . . hey, Bill! C'mere!'

From the other side of the airlock compartment, a young man's head popped through the open hatch – upside-down, at least to my frame of reference. 'Yeah, Dad?' he said. 'I'm kinda busy at the moment . . . Kaneko didn't stow his suit properly.'

The elder William silently cocked a forefinger, summoning his son into the compartment. He was not a man who accepted no for an answer. William Tate-Smith, Jr – usually known aboard ship as Young Bill – reluctantly pushed himself into the airlock from the adjacent storage compartment. 'Bill, this is Elliot Cole,' his father said. 'He's the writer Saul told us about.'

Young Bill was like a sixteen-year-old version of his first-father, except in place of a beard he sported a long, brown braid of hair. He was also much taller than his dad; just a couple of centimetres shy of two metres, with the narrow-waisted, slender-limbed build of a young man born and bred in space. Floating next to the man who helped conceive him – a man who had been raised on Earth – he looked like a beansprout next to a tuber.

'Hey! Glad to meet you, Mr Cole.' Young Bill was still upside-down – perhaps deliberately so, trying to see if he can shake me up a little with his display of zero-gee gymnastics – but he eagerly stuck out his hand. I fumbled to shake it and instead lost my grip on a ceiling rung and tumbled forward; he grinned mischievously, confirming my suspicions.

'Read your last book, the one about the Brazilian reforestation project,' he said. 'Thought it was pretty bucho. Maybe we can talk later about the . . .'

'Later,' his father said impatiently, giving him a stern look. 'Right now, I want you to take Mr Cole's bag to his compartment, then escort him up to the bridge. I'll call Kaneko down here and have him put away his suit.' Young Bill solemnly nodded his head. Clearly there was no arguing with his old man . . . and judging from the expression on William Smith-Tate's face, I would not have liked to be Kaneko. whoever he was, when he answered to the chief engineer's wrath.

The teenager silently reached around me to grab the strap of my duffle bag from my shoulder, then he executed a perfect midair somersault and, with youthful grace which looked almost effortless, swam back toward the compartment hatch, hauling my bag behind him. I looked around again to thank William Smith-Tate, but he had already turned away, pushing shut the airlock hatch and spinning the lockwheel to dog it shut. He bent to the round window next to the hatch and gave a short wave to the shuttle pilot, then he pressed his right hand against his jaw and murmured something unintelligible. For a moment I thought that he was grumbling to himself, until I realized that he was talking to someone elsewhere in the ship, using the nanomike which had been surgically implanted beneath his skin.

There was another soft thud as the shuttle disengaged from the ship's docking collar; through the window, I could see the navigation beacons of the smaller vessel as it silently moved away. Now there was truly no turning back: for better or for worse, I was aboard the *Medici Explorer* for keeps.

The distraction caused me to fall behind Young Bill, and he didn't wait for me. I hastened to catch up with him, grabbing at rungs in the ceiling to haul myself through the adjacent compartment. The narrow bulkheads were lined with recessed lockers – each stencilled with the name of one of the ship's ten crewmembers – and racks containing hardsuit helmets, utility belts and miscellaneous spare suit parts. The EVA ready-room, like the airlock, is quite utilitarian, although very clean and dust-free; the discipline necessary for space travel mandates that nothing be left out of place.

Almost nothing. The sole exception was one half-open locker, with the legs and one sleeve of an empty hardsuit sticking out. I was surprised to see that it was quite small.

Young Bill stopped to wait for me on the other side of the ready-room. He floated in an open vertical shaft, one hand gripping the top rung of a ladder, the other holding the strap of my duffel bag over his shoulder; he had taken the trouble to make himself right-side up. 'I really mean it,' he began as he pushed himself down the shaft, 'I loved *Rain Forest Diary* . . . it was really lollapalooza . . . I almost had a cardiac when the Captain told me that the dude who wrote it was coming with us . . . maybe you can tell me some more, y'know, about the Brazilian indians and the . . .'

So on and so forth, barely pausing for breath, as we dropped down the hub's access shaft to the carousel which connects the hub to the ship's three arms. Since the arms were not presently rotating, we didn't need to make the tricky manoeuvre of reorienting ourselves until the appropriate hatchway swung past us. The carousel's hatches were aligned with their appropriate arms, so all we had to do was squirm through the upward-bending corridor – passing the sealed tiger-striped hatch which led to the reactor stack in Arm Three – until we reached the open hatch marked 'ARM 1'.

The arm's central shaft resembled a deep well, fifteen metres straight down to the bottom. Although I consciously knew that I couldn't fall into zero-gee, I instinctively rebelled at the thought of throwing myself into a neck-breaking plummet. While I hesitated at the edge of the abyss, Young Bill dove headfirst through the hatch, scarcely grabbing the rungs of the ladder which led down the blue-carpeted wall of the shaft. I shut my eyes for a moment, fighting a surge of nausea, then I eased myself feet-first into the shaft, carefully taking each rung a step at a time.

There are six levels in Arm One, each accessed by the long ladder. Still babbling happily about rain forests and South American Indian tribes, Young Bill led me past Level 1-A (the infirmary and life sciences lab) Level 1-B (the Smith-Tate residence), Level 1-C (Smith-Makepeace) and Level 1-D (Smith-Tanaka). The hatches to each deck were shut, but as we glided past Level 1-D, its hatch opened and a preadolescent boy recklessly rushed out into the shaft and almost collided with Young Bill.

'Whoa there!' Young Bill gently grabbed the child by his shoulders, braking him before he could slam into either one of us. 'Watch yourself, OK?'

'Sorry.' The youngster reached out and took hold of a rung of the ladder, righting himself in midair. Judging from his apparent age, he was Kaneko Smith-Tanaka, the youngest member of the crew: four years old, going on five. Like Young Bill, he was taller and more slender than other children his age: the elfin physiology of the space-born.

His oriental face was very determined. 'I need to get up to 2-H 'cause Uncle Bill is mad at me because I . . .'

'Didn't put your suit away like you were supposed to.' Young Bill, still holding on to Kaneko's shoulders, stared straight into the boy's eyes. 'And I'm the one who noticed, not Uncle Bill. Aren't you a little too old to be doing this sort of thing?'

Kaneko looked embarrassed; his gaze moved down toward his moccasined toes, dangling five metres above the bottom of the access shaft. Like his older 'brother', Kaneko thought no more of freefall than a child on Earth considers a flight of stairs; zero-gee was simply a fact of life, nothing more nor less. 'And if you don't put your suit away,' Young Bill adds, 'who will, hmm? Me? Somebody else?'

'Maybe . . .' Kaneko began haltingly, then his face suddenly brightened. 'Maybe Ditz can do it!'

'Ditz . . .?' Young Bill glanced away from Kaneko, peering through the open hatch of the Smith-Tanaka quarters. 'Aw, jeez . . . Ditz, are you in there?'

6

There was a mechanical scuttling sound from within the hatch, then a tinny electronic voice announced itself: '*Ditz here! Ditz here!*'

A small robot, resembling a hermit crab but slightly larger than a housecat, abruptly scurried into sight, secured to the deck by the stikpads at the ends of its six tiny legs. A discarded plastic squeezebulb was held between its pincers. '*Look what Ditz found!*' it said proudly. '*Good trash! See? See?*'

Kaneko giggled with childish delight. Young Bill sighed. 'That's very good, Ditz,' he told the autonomous intelligence. 'Now go put it in the recycle chute and continue cleaning this Arm, please.'

Ditz went chattering away, proudly clutching the prized squeezebulb, and Young Bill looked again at his clan-brother. 'Kaneko, Ditz isn't a pet. It's an AI . . . you can't keep it in your room all the time. And it's too small to put away your hardsuit for you. That's your responsibility. Understand?'

The child solemnly nodded his head, looking down at his feet again. 'OK then,' Young Bill said. 'Now go up there and put away your suit before Uncle Bill gets mad, then get yourself to the bridge. We're getting close to launch.'

Kaneko Smith-Tanaka silently pushed off from the ladder, gliding past Young Bill and me; he barely glanced in my direction, apparently incurious about who I was or why I was in his home. Young Bill was about to shut the hatch to the Tanaka deck when Ditz reappeared.

'*Kaneko, wait for Ditz!*' it squealed as it hastily clambered around the hatchway and began crawling up the ladder. Kaneko stopped, his smile reappearing as the tiny robot raced to catch up with him; together, the boy and his adopted playmate headed up the shaft.

'Wouldn't a cat be more appropriate?' I whispered as we watched them leave the Arm through the carousel hatch.

Young Bill shook his head. 'Naw . . . cats can't handle freefall. We used to have one when we lived on the Moon, but Dad wouldn't let us bring it aboard the ship. He says the fur gets into everything.' Young Bill shut the hatch, then led me down one more level to Deck 1-E, the passenger quarters. 'At least he isn't playing with Swamp anymore. That's the galley AI . . . things used to get messy when they'd play in the sink together.'

He opened the hatch to Deck 1-E and pulled himself inside, hauling my duffel bag behind him. The deck is divided into four passenger staterooms, along with a common bathroom; not surprisingly, it was marked 'HEAD', retaining the old nautical term. The small compartment Bill led me to had its own foldaway bed, desk, data terminal and screen, along with a wide square window through which I could see the Moon.

'Don't bother making yourself at home,' he said as he stowed my duffel bag in a closet. 'After we launch, you won't see this place again for nine months.'

I nodded. 'The other passengers . . . they're already in hibernation?'

'Yep. I helped Uncle Yoshi dope 'em up a few hours ago. They're zombified already. You'll be joining them after we . . .'

He stopped abruptly in mid-sentence, listening to something through his nanolink, then he pressed the right side of his jaw. 'I've got him here with me, Uncle Geoff. We're coming right now . . . yeah, OK. Be there in a minute.'

Young Bill shut the closet door and pushed past me toward the compartment door. 'That was my uncle. We're wanted on the bridge. Captain's initiated the final countdown . . . we're out of here in thirty minutes.'

I took one last look at my quarters, then turned around to exit the compartment. Bill had already left the passenger deck and was climbing the ladder up the shaft toward the hub, leaving me to close the deck hatch myself. One fact was already being made abundantly clear to me; aboard the *Medici Explorer*, everyone was expected to pull their own weight. No excuses were accepted – not for youth, nor for unfamiliarity with the ship.

The *Medici Explorer*'s command centre is shaped like the inside of a Chinese wok. Located on the top deck of the hub, Deck H-1 is the largest single compartment in the vessel: about fifteen metres in diameter, the bridge has a sloping, dome-shaped ceiling above a shallow, tiered pit. Two observation blisters, each containing an optical telescope, are mounted in the ceiling at opposite ends of the pit; between them are myriad computer flatscreens and holographic displays, positioned above the duty stations arranged around the circumference of the pit. In the centre of the bridge, at the bottom of the pit between and slightly below the duty stations, is the captain's wingbacked chair, surrounded by wraparound consoles. On one side of the bridge is the hatch leading to the hub's access tunnel; on the opposite side is a small alcove, a rest area furnished with three chairs and a small galley.

It may sound claustrophobic, but the bridge is actually quite spacious and comfortable. The floors are carpeted, allowing one to comfortably walk on them provided that you're wearing stikshoes, and the holoscreens provide a variety of scenes from outboard cameras as well as the main telescope, giving the illusion of cathedral windows looking out upon the grand cosmos.

But now, in the last few minutes before departure from near-Earth space, the command centre was indeed crowded; the entire Smith clan, along with the captain, was gathered in the bridge, making ready to commence the journey. After Young Bill and I paused in the foyer to slip on stikshoes, he led me into the bridge and quickly introduced me to his family. No one had a chance to do much more than smile and give me a polite, hurried greeting; everyone was absorbed in their last-minute tasks.

Seated at the navigation console was Elizabeth Smith-Makepeace, a thin young woman in her mid-thirties; she barely glanced away from her console, not distracting herself from entering triaxial co-ordinates into her computer terminal as she intently watched several flatscreens which showed the ship's outbound trajectory. At the communications station next to her was her first-husband, Geoffery Smith-Makepeace, a tall, gaunt man with a lantern jaw; he too was concentrating wholly upon his job, talking to lunar traffic controllers while relaying pertinent information to the captain.

On the opposite side of the bridge, seated on either side of the passenger alcove, were William Smith-Tate – he gave me a brief stare before returning his attention to his checklist of the engineering station – and Leslie Smith-Tanaka, a very attractive woman with grey-streaked brown hair. The life-support chief flashed me a dazzling smile as I walked past; her troublesome son Kaneko stood next to her, watching over her shoulder as his mother ran through her own checklist.

Seated next to Leslie was Lynn Smith-Tate, a muscular woman with a perpetual scowl which almost matched her first-husband's; as hydroponics chief, she was also absorbed with making sure that the life-support systems are functioning properly, particularly the hydroponics decks in Arm Two. It was difficult to imagine that such an easy-going teenager as Young Bill could be the offspring of such stoical parents. The only relaxed crewmember seemed to be Yoshio Smith-Tanaka, the ship's physician, a short, rotund Japanese man with grey hair and an eternally calm disposition. He stood next to the captain's chair while silently watching everything going on around him.

And then there was Saul Montrose, the captain himself. The only crewmember who wasn't part of the extended family, he was tall and rail-thin, a trim black beard easing the taut jawline of his dark face. Not much else of his face could be seen; his head was incased in a VR helmet, his data-gloved hands moving in midair as he manipulated invisible controls in cyberspace.

Young Bill guided me to the rest alcove, where I met the last member of the Smith clan: Wendy Smith-Makepeace, eight years old, a little replica of her mother Betsy (although, like Bill and Kaneko, taller and thinner than most of her contemporaries on Earth). She watched me with silent appraisal as I took a seat next to her, as seemingly indifferent to my presence as her half-brother Taneko before her – then, as I fumbled with the seat belt, she reached over and, in one fluid motion, expertly tightened the strap and snapped shut the buckle.

'If you don't know how to do it,' she lectured me sternly, 'ask someone.' Then she primly folded her hands in her lap and stoically looked straight ahead, watching her first-parents across the compartment.

'I'll leave you to Wendy's tender mercy,' Young Bill said as he gave me a slap on the shoulder. He then pushed off the floor, floating upward to grab a ceiling rung. 'Captain, may I watch the launch from the blister, please?'

It didn't seem as if Montrose could hear anything from within his thick VR helmet, but the captain circled a thumb and index finger, giving him the OK sign. 'Thank you, sir,' Young Bill said, then worked his way along the ceiling rungs, hand over hand, until he reached the observation blister between the engineering and communications stations. With one free hand he tapped the control panel next to the hemispherical bulge; the blister's hatch slid open, briefly revealing a tiny compartment with a single armchair mounted in front of a binocular eyepiece. Young Bill glided feet-first into the blister, then the hatch shut behind him.

It was now very calm within the command centre, almost silent except for the low murmur of voices. Since everyone communicated through their subcutaneous comlink, there was none of the melodramatic shouting across the bridge usually depicted in net space dramas. I found a headset stowed in a basket beneath my seat; after fiddling with it for a few moments, I was able to monitor the overlapping crosstalk.

'T-minus twenty minutes and counting . . .'

'Tank pressurization check complete, all levels stable . . .'

'Cycle primary guidance system to on my mark to delta three-three-two . . .'

'Copy, delta three-three-two . . .'

'Telemetry check clear. Tycho DSR says we are green, repeat, green for go . . .'

'Mark for primary guidance sequence initiation . . .'

'Roger that. Stand by for main engine reactor sequence. Ten per cent fuel feed on my mark at T-minus fifteen, counting . . .'

A new voice came over the comlink: *'Ah, one-twelve Whisky Bravo Nebraska, this is Descartes Traffic, we've got a vessel three hundred klicks downrange from your trajectory. Nine-nine-one Nebraska Foxtrot Omega bearing X-ray fifteen, Yankee eleven-point-six, Zulu minus oh-one, please hold until we can move it from your lane. Over.'*

'We copy, Descartes Traffic,' Captain Montrose said, *'but we're not holding on the burn till we confirm, over. Betsy, you want to hop on that, please?'*

Elizabeth Smith-Makepeace checked her navigation screens and discovered that 991-NFO was a cargo carrier out of Clarke County, the LaGrangian colony. The barge was close to 112-WBN's flight path, but not so much as to directly endanger any of the convoy's ships with direct collision.

Montrose sighed, barely nodding his head; it was a momentary nuisance, not a crisis. *'Descartes Traffic, this is one-twelve Whisky Bravo Nebraska, please be advised that we are initiating reactor warm-up and preparing for JOI burn. If we go into hold now, we're gonna miss our window, so please inform the pilot . . .'*

'One-twelve Whisky Bravo Nebraska, this is Descartes Traffic. Don't worry, we've taken care of it. Nine-nine-one Nebraska Foxtrot Omega is adjusting its course to take itself out of your lane and its pilot renders his apologies. Over.'

'Thank you, Descartes Traffic. One-twelve Whisky Bravo Nebraska green for launch. Over.' The voice of Descartes Traffic vanished from the comlink.

'Ready for primary engine ignition sequence on your mark . . .'

'Mark on three . . . one, two, and three . . .'

There was a faint surge through the mammoth ship as the gas-core reactor rumbled to life, its hydrogen fuel passing through conduits into the giant main engine at the far end of the ship. Digital readouts on Bill Smith-Tate's console flashed from red to green; he hardly seemed to notice as his hands moved quickly from one touchpad to the next. *'Standing by to initiate pressurization of secondary engines.'*

'Go for secondary engine pressurization,' Montrose said, and Old Bill complied. The liquid-fuel engines which comprised the ship's manoeuvring thrusters were made ready for launch. *'OK, prepare for Arm rotation intiation, on my mark at one . . .'*

Montrose's hands flitted around in midair, pressing invisible buttons only he could see. Although he had final command over every major decision in the countdown, he depended on the rest of his crew to give him information that would confirm what he saw in cyberspace; too many things can go wrong in virtual reality, and their feedback was necessary as an anchor to real-life.

'Three . . . two . . . one and mark . . .' Now the vessel's three arms began to slowly rotate around the hub, gradually running up to the two RPMs which would induce one-tenth gravity within the habitation areas. There was an initial sense of swerving movement through the hull until the main computer automatically fired RCRs to compensate for the torque, then the rocking motion gradually faded.

It was now ten minutes until launch. The crew moved through the rest of the checklist. Final telemetry tests with the three drone freighters, making sure they were slaved to the *Medici Explorer's* guidance system and primed for simultaneous launch. A run-through of the seven back-up computers in search of unexpected bugs and glitches. Double-checking the fuselage sensors for airleaks, confirming that the inside hatches had all been secured. Running a systems-test of the primary life-support mainframe to ascertain that all the temperature, humidity, and oxygen-nitrogen feeds were up to par. All done with calm, unhurried competence, almost as if this bewildering array of chores was being performed in a ConSpace training simulator.

By the time the engine-arm sequence was initiated at T-minus two minutes, however, a thin sheen of sweat had appeared on Old Bill's forehead. Yoshio Smith-Tanaka moved from the captain's station to a bulkhead on the upper tier where he took firm hold of a pair of rungs, and Leslie Smith-Tanaka quietly told Kaneko to take a seat in the passenger alcove. The child was grinning unabashedly as he unerringly kicked across the compartment toward Wendy Smith-Makepeace and myself; the girl reached up and snagged Kaneko, hauling him into the chair next to her and strapping him down.

'*T-minus-sixty seconds,*' Montrose said. '*All systems on auto-exec, burn in fifty seconds. Descartes Traffic, this is the* Medici Explorer, *one-twelve Whisky Bravo Nebraska, requesting final launch clearance. Over.*'

'*One-twelve Whisky Bravo Nebraska, this is Descartes Traffic, you have permission to launch when ready.* Via con dios *and good luck. Over.*'

'*Thank you, Descartes Traffic. See you when we get back. Over and out.*' Montrose settled back in his seat, his hands lightly resting on the arms of his chair. '*Burn minus five . . . four . . . three . . . two . . . one . . .*'

Now there was a great tremor through the ship, a miniature earthquake over three thousand kilometers from the nearest geological fault, as the primary engine surged to life. On one of the holoscreens, a camera mounted on the outer hull caught a glimpse of a brilliant white-hot flare erupting aft of the radiation shield, as if a tactical nuke had exploded behind the *Medici Explorer*. There was no noise, no great roar – only a dull rumble which was felt more than heard, as everyone grasped their armrests, feeling the anticipated haul of gravity, the weight which pushed them firmly in their padded seats.

'*Hot shit!*' The voice belonged to Young Bill, yelling over the comlink from the observation blister. '*Move, baby, move . . . !*'

Then the secondary engines kicked in, gradually easing the *Medici Explorer* out of the Moon's shallow gravity well, as the ship's computers guided the vessel toward deep space. There was the almost-imperceptible sensation of rising. The hull creaked softly as bulkhead joists moved together. On one screen, the Moon began to gradually fall away; on another, Earth canted sideways, as if the planet itself had changed orbit by a few degrees.

'*I love it, I love it, I love it!*' Young Bill was shouting. '*I can feel you movin', baby! I can feel you humpin'* . . . !'

'*Watch your mouth, boy!*' his father snapped and Young Bill abruptly fell silent, yet there were quiet, knowing grins throughout the bridge. On other screens, small flares of light from port and starboard showed that the engines of the three freighters had also fired, following the *Medici Explorer* as the convoy began to move out of lunar orbit.

It was 10 January 2061. We were on our way to Jupiter, the largest of all explored worlds, king of the solar system. From here to there, there were 628,700,000 kilometres of space . . . .

And the weight.

The Jupiter Run

THE REASONS WHY the *Medici Explorer* again set sail for Jupiter and the Galilean moons, when analysed closely, have less to do with the exploration of the cosmos than with the politics and problems of the last one hundred years. Although Jupiter has been regaled as the latest frontier of humankind's 'conquest of space' – itself a romantic term, as witnessed by the current spate of adventure fiction set in the Jovian system, most of it woefully inaccurate – the rationale behind the so-called 'Jupiter Run' is principally grounded in historical events which go as far back as the last decades of the twentieth century.

Until 2037, there was little practical reason for anyone to visit Jupiter. Its sheer distance from Earth – 4.2 astronomical units, or about 628,700,000 kilometres – made it almost inconceivable of being efficiently reached with liquid-fuel rockets. When the first unmanned probe from Earth to Jupiter, NASA's *Pioneer 10*, swung past the planet in December 1973, it confirmed that the miniature solar system orbiting the world was a realm of both great beauty and great danger; Jupiter was surrounded by menacing radiation belts ten thousand times more lethal than the Van Allen belt around Earth. Subsequent unmanned space missions – *Pioneer 11*, the two Voyagers later in the same decade and the *Galileo* probe during the 1990s – took closer looks at the Galilean moons; however fascinating they were, none looked particularly habitable. Only science fiction writers continued to seriously dream of manned spacecraft to Jupiter. For scientists, the Jovian system was something to be studied from a safe distance, visited only by robotic proxy.

However, this attitude gradually changed in the next century. With the beginning of the 'Golden Age' of space exploration – the building of the powersat system, the colonization of the Moon and the establishment of the first bases on Mars – Jupiter began to look neither so distant nor so formidable. The major technological breakthrough which made Jupiter reachable was made in 2028 by a joint R&D project by Russian and American physicists at the Kurchatov Institute of Atomic Energy and the Lawrence Livermore National Laboratory: the development of a gas-core nuclear engine, resulting in an impulse-per-second engine thrust ratio twice as high as even the thermal-fission engines used by Mars cycleships.

Jupiter beckoned, and humankind followed. Under the auspices of the newly formed International Space Commission, with funding provided by several private-sector space companies, the first manned Jupiter vessel, the *Tycho Brahe*, was built in Earth orbit. Its ten-person crew voyaged to Jupiter in 2037, returning to Earth in 2039, nineteen months after departure, with enough new scientific information about the Jovian system to fill a small library. However, despite the fact that a small base camp had been established – and abandoned – on Callisto, the fourth major Galilean moon, there seemed to be little reason to colonize Jupiter. It seemed as if humankind was permanently destined to inhabit only the inner solar system; common sense seemed to dictate that Jupiter, as academically intriguing as it was, served no immediate practical use for the human race.

'When the Sun dies,' said the esteemed British astrophysicist Shelly Wood, 'we may have good motive for settling Callisto or Ganymede. Until then, I'm quite satisfied to keep my current address in London.' Thus would remain the conventional wisdom for the next fifteen years, until the Moon War of 2052 proved that the human race could not afford to remain stagnant within the inner solar system.

By 2032, the first few large-scale fusion plants were in operation in the United States and Japan. By 2052, more than five hundred commercial tokamaks were being used around the world. Nuclear fusion had successfully supplanted the fossil-fuel plants of the twentieth century and even the powersats of the early twenty-first as the major energy resource for most of the industrialized world. The fuel source which made their operation possible was helium-3, an isotope which was extremely rare on Earth but abundant on the Moon . . . and since there seemed to be infinite supplies of helium-3 trapped within the Moon's regolith, conventional wisdom held that this was a resource which could be mined, refined and shipped home until the Sun did indeed grow cold.

However, yesterday's wisdom often turns out to be tomorrow's misguided thinking. When the lunar settlement at Descartes Station, prompted by the Clarke County space colony's declaration of independence, also decreed itself to be a sovereign state, the governments and corporations which had previously thought helium-3 to be an infinitely exploitable resource, free to be extracted by whoever had the ability to put the necessary hardware on the Moon, suddenly found themselves facing new political realities. It was a situation remarkably similar to that faced by the Western countries and oil companies of the twentieth century when the Arab nations of the Middle East realized their true power and flexed their muscles, resulting in revolutions, embargoes and wars. The defeat of American-Russian space forces in the Battle of Mare Tranquilitatis in 2052, and the subsequent establishment of the Pax Astra by the free countries of Clarke County and Descartes City, forced the terrestrial nations to come to grips with the fact that lunar helium-3 was no longer cheap nor endlessly available.

The tokamaks of the Americas, Europe, Africa and Asia had to be fed or the wheels of civilization would grind to a halt, and the price of lunar helium-3 was not getting any cheaper. Even after the post-war tariffs were relaxed, following formal recognition of the Pax Astra by the United Nations, establishment of much of the lunar nearside as protected wilderness areas made it necessary for the government–industrial apparatus on Earth to look elsewhere for long-term energy reserves.

It had been known for almost a century that Jupiter's upper atmosphere was rich with helium-3. In fact, not only was the isotope more abundant on Jupiter than on the Moon, but since it was not molecularly bound with all the other elements found in lunar regolith, it was theoretically easier to extract. As far back as the 1970s, the British Interplanetary Society had proposed 'mining' Jupiter's atmosphere for helium-3, although its projected purpose had been to serve as fuel for the proposed *Daedelus* unmanned interstellar probe. It didn't take long for Consolidated Space Industries – the new independent consortium formed between Skycorp, Uchu-Hiko, Galileo Inc. and several other space companies – to dust off the old BIS scheme and see that it was not only technologically feasible, but in the long run more economically sound than depending entirely upon lunar helium-3.

Over the next ten years, ConSpace invested heavily in a crash programme to begin Jovian mining operations. It was a mammoth undertaking, made even more remarkable by the speed in which it was accomplished. When the *Tycho Brahe* returned to Jupiter in 2057, it carried with it the first atmospheric separation plant. The nuclear-powered, remote-controlled system was dropped from low-orbit into the planet's upper atmosphere, where it inflated immense balloon-like aerostats which countered the gravitational pull. *Prometheus 1* then commenced to automatically siphon helium-3 from the swirling cloudtops as it was whisked around the planet by the upper-atmospheric jetstreams, liquifying it and storing it in outboard tanks, which drone rockets would eventually launch out of the planet's gravity well. The *Brahe* then ventured out to Callisto, where additional modules were brought down to the abandoned base camp which the first expedition had left in the Valhalla Basin, the first step in expanding the temporary camp into a permanent habitat.

At the same time, four new deep-space vessels – the *Medici Explorer*, as well as its drone freighters – were being built in lunar orbit. The *Medici Explorer* (named after the Medici family of Renaissance Italy, the patrons of Galileo Galilei's research) was essentially a sister-ship of the *Tycho Brahe*, with upgraded engines and more spacious crew and passenger compartments. The freighters were simplified versions of the same design, each substituting a massive payload sphere for the hub-and-arm configuration. Another similiar space vessel, the *Herschel Explorer*, was already on the drawing-board, and long-range plans called a fleet of three Brahe-class ships, along with their freighters, to eventually rotate between Earth and Jupiter, similar to the cycleships which linked Earth and Mars.

Their swift construction was made possible by a co-operative agreement reached between the Pax Astra and ConSpace. In return for supplying lunar-made shipbuilding materials and portside facilities and services, ConSpace would share a pro-rated per cent of its eventual profits with Descartes Station and Clarke County. Although Jovian helium-3 undercut the market for lunar helium-3, the Pax was wise enough to take the longer view: the agreement not only gave it a new economic base, since the Moon would be the terminus for future flights to Jupiter, but it would also help preserve the Moon's resources. It also helped the space colonies to achieve political reconciliation with their former governments on Earth; both the United States and Japan had been threatening an embargo on lunar-made products, and the Pax didn't want to risk losing the independence for which it had fought so long and hard.

And then, just as success was at everyone's fingertips, one of the greatest disasters in the history of manned space exploration occurred: the loss of the *Tycho Brahe*.

Only three members of the second expedition survived the vessel's freak-accident collision with a boulder-sized rock as the *Brahe* was journeying through the asteroid belt on its way back to Earth. It was partly as a result of their testimony in front of the International Space Commission, during which the causes for the loss of the seven other cosmonauts were fully explained, that a new methodology was established for the selection of the crews of the *Medici Explorer* and all other Jovian ships to follow.

According to the survivors of the *Tycho Brahe*, the true reason why so many lives were lost had little to do with the fact that their vessel had been struck by a small asteroid. Indeed, the collision could have been avoided, and should have been; in hindsight, it was the human factor which had doomed the ship, not the asteroid itself.

When ConSpace had selected the crew for the *Brahe*'s second voyage, it was almost strictly on the basis of either astronautical or scientific skills; in their rush to get the ship underway, little forethought had been given by the mission's planning team to balancing the crew on a psychological basis. As a result, the crew had all the expertise needed to perform their assignments, but they were also socially mismatched: seven men, three women, all of whom were either single or not very stably married.

To further add to the mess, there was disparity between the ship's command crew, who thought of the *Brahe* as their domain and the scientists who were aboard as passengers, whose know-ledge was vital but who came to be treated as second-class citizens. It was never clearly delineated who was in command, the captain or the senior mission scientist. Which was more important, the horse or the cart? No one really knew who was in charge; as a result, during the long months of the flight, a schism grew between the people in the command centre and the people in the labs.

Added to this was a singles-bar atmosphere, due to the sexual mismatch of the crew members. The question of who was sleeping with whom often became more important than the mission objectives. Tempers flared, tensions rose, cliques formed which stalled command decisions . . . and meanwhile, mundane chores such as galley clean-up and routine shipboard repairs were left undone.

The *Tycho Brahe* managed to perform its objectives, but by the time the vessel left Jupiter and began its long journey home, half of its crew were no longer on speaking terms with the other half. It didn't seem to matter very much by then – the scientists and engineers were asleep in zombie tanks for the ride home – but the crewmembers who had not gone into hibernation became slovenly in carrying out their regular duties.

The tiny asteroid which collided with the *Brahe* could, and should, have been detected by whoever was supposed to be standing watch in the bridge. Given warning, the crew might have corrected the ship's course in time to avoid collision. However, the crewmembers who were supposed to be on watch were in the hydroponics area instead, squabbling over whose turn it was to monitor the nutrient feedlines. When the rock slammed into Arm Two, three levels below them and just above the hibernation bay, emergency hatches should have closed immediately, sealing off each level and limiting the extent of the catastrophe. However, someone had neglected to reset the circuit breaker which controlled the hatches, so the entire Arm was blown out.

Two errors, both avoidable had the crew not been paralysed by interpersonal conflict. As a result, all five persons in hibernation, plus the two crewmates in the hydroponics area, were killed by the asteroid collision. Only three crewmembers who had been asleep in their quarters in Arm One at the time escaped death.

The survivors managed to patch the *Tycho Brahe* together just enough to get them as far as Mars orbit, where they were ultimately forced to abandon ship and make their way to the red planet in the ship's boat. The *Brahe* itself went into an elongated solar orbit; it wasn't until three years later that it was retrieved by a salvage team from Arsia Station, who brought the derelict back to Mars as scrap metal.

Despite the tragedy and the setback it posed, ConSpace pressed on with its plans to open helium-mining operations in Jovian space. Yet the loss of seven lives, plus a valuable ship, forced the consortium to reconsider the means by which future crews of its deep-space vessels would be chosen.

In that sense, the *Brahe* disaster was a blessing, because it finally coerced technocrats to ponder long-overlooked problems of human behaviour during long space missions. As far back as the 1980s, these questions had been posed by those who studied space flight, even though the major space agencies – most typically NASA, which had habitually short-changed life sciences in favour of hardware development – had typically swept them under the rug. The *Brahe* disaster was vivid testimony to the fact that the human condition was a more complex problem than could be solved by choosing pastel colours for the living quarters or putting in another porthole for sightseeing. Engineers and executives alike were impelled to come away from their blueprints and spreadsheets and listen to the psychologists, and what they were told was that the makeup of crews for long-duration flights was at least as important as IPS ratios and orbital mechanics.

What the psychologists told them, in fact, was that, in terms of social order, the most stable social groups were families. If they wanted to make sure that no more *Brahe* disasters occurred in the future, they would do well to put entire families in space. And since ten-person families, in which all the members had the necessary expertise to serve aboard a deep-space vessel, were practically impossible to find, the only available recourse was to generate them.

Fortunately, this had already been done.

The concept of extended families is not new to the human race but, with few exceptions, the practice has been frowned upon, if not made illegal, in Western civilization. Yet when intermarriage re-emerged during the formation of the first self-sufficient colonies on the Moon and Mars, the long-standing Judeo-Christian mores against polygamy were forced to take a back seat to practicality.

The first space colonists didn't have to worry about raising families on the high frontier. They were, for the most part, itinerant blue-collar labourers who had signed temporary contracts with the major space companies, leaving their spouses and children at home to fend for themselves for a year or two while they went to work in near-Earth orbit or on the Moon.

Indeed, the first married couple did not journey together into space until 1992, and that was almost by accident; NASA had assigned two astronauts to a shuttle flight, then had to watch in chagrin as they exchanged wedding vows before their mission. Even after that, however, it remained the policy of first NASA, then later the private space companies, not to allow married partners in space, under the theory that a couple could disrupt crew morale. Visions of wild orbital orgies danced in the puritanical minds of too many officials, who refused to believe that love, or at least normal sexual urges, could coexist with The Conquest of Space. 'One in the sky, one on the ground' was the unspoken rule of thumb.

The same went for unplanned pregnancies, and even more so. Female crewmembers were sometimes knocked up, usually the outcome of one-night stands. Rules against sex were virtually unenforceable, but being preggers was; the inevitable result of getting in the family way was either that the woman lost her job but went back to Earth to have a baby, or kept her job but had an abortion. Keeping both the job and the kid was not an available alternative.

This began to change when Lunar Associates Ltd. was established in 2024 as an employee-owned company; Descartes Station was now controlled not by corporate suits on Earth but by its own workers. As a result, there was now an economic incentive for 'moondogs' to become permanent settlers rather than temporary labourers . . . and it wasn't long before many of Descartes Station's employee-stockholders demanded the right to marry and have children.

Marriage was widely considered to be OK . . . but kids? It took long and impassioned debate among the lunar colonists, but in the end the old Skycorp regulations were voted out of LA's charter (although a one-child-per-family rule was put firmly in place) and on 1 April 2025, Mary Selene Rosenkrantz made history by being the first child to be born beyond the planet Earth.

Mary wasn't unique for very long. Very soon she had many other kids to play with, and this opened yet another can of worms. Finding good day-care has been one of the vexing problems of the ages. Since everyone on the Moon was expected to work for a living, this made finding a reliable babysitter once every three shifts a major obstacle.

Simultaneously, there was also the problem of rampant adultery among the colonists. With only a hundred and fifty people in Descartes Station, all living together in close quarters, there was strong temptation for even the closest of couples to have secret extramarital affairs with other persons. As the colony prospered, its population rose, but by the time Descartes Station was officially renamed Descartes City, wives often found themselves sleeping with their best friend's husbands and vice versa, sometimes while their kids were romping in the very next compartment. Even after there were the inevitable discoveries, quarrels, separations, and tearful make-ups, the trend continued, leading many to observe that the social atmosphere within Descartes City had begun to resemble an ongoing soap opera, only without theme music and commercial breaks.

The solution to both problems found itself in 2031 when three families – the Phillipses, the Freys, and the Horowitzes – came to the mutual epiphany that they didn't mind so much the fact that they were fooling around with each other's spouses as they did the betrayal of trust that went along with it. This together with the realization that their babies didn't really seem to care who was at home at what time, so long as their diapers continued to be changed and they were regularly nourished. Since none of the three couples had any strong religious feelings against the idea, the families decided to cut the Gordian knot by tying a different one altogether: they presented themselves to Descartes City's resident priest, the Revd Luther Paulsen, and demanded to be intermarried.

When Paulsen, a Presbyterian minister who was also the station's chief dietician, refused to condone the intermarriage, they found a bulldozer driver who was a licensed Justice of the Peace. He listened to their reasons for intermarriage and agreed to officiate, and thus the three families were married together in a public ceremony conducted in the station greenhouse. Rather than have their surnames changed to one couple's last name, or to have an unwieldy three-way hyphenated surname, the clan randomly selected a neutral name – Jones – to be their shared title. Therefore, they became the Jones-Phillips, Jones-Frey, Jones-Horowitz family. In short, the Joneses.

As bizarre as it initially seemed, the concept of clanish inter-marriage soon caught on. It gave greater stability to pre-existent two-person marriages, eased the problem of raising children, and virtually eliminated the eternal question of whose turn it was to take out the garbage. Although at first it was done only on the Moon, the practice soon spread to Clarke County and the Arsia Station colony on Mars. Polygamy was still technically illegal, but when so many people started participating in multi-partner marriages, the colony governments couldn't do much more than look the other way.

Following the Moon War and the formation of the Pax Astra, polygamy was formally legalized on the Moon and in Clarke County, as the 11th Amendment of the Pax's Bill of Rights. This had the unanticipated side-effect of luring a new breed of colonists into space – the so-called 'jack-Mormons'. Although the Church of Latter-Day Saints officially condemned the polygamy as inherently sinful, the Mormons had virtually pioneered the concept of intermarriage before it was outlawed in the United States in the 1800s. Even so, quite a few jack-Mormons continued to secretly practice intermarriage, and when polygamy was made legal in the Pax Astra, many of them migrated to space. There they not only practiced polygamy without fear of criminal prosecution, but also won converts to the Church among the clans which felt the need for spiritual guidance.

This caused considerable debate within the Church's upper hierarchy, since it opened a hellish conundrum: either all those jack-Mormons in the Pax had to be excommunicated from the Church, although what they were practicing was completely legal and they were rapidly gaining new converts to the faith, or the Church had to officially sanction polygamy despite its earlier admonishments. In the end, the Church's leadership had a divine revelation in which God said it was OK for polygamy to be practiced 'within certain situations in an extraterrestrial environment'.

By the time ConSpace began selecting crews for the Jupiter Run, there were quite a few extended families on the Moon, Mars and

Clarke County from which to choose. The first of these to be selected, as the crew of the newly christened *Medici Explorer*, was the Smith family of Descartes City.

This decision didn't come as an accident or as the result of favouritism or clout. The Smiths were chosen because they were stable, they were tough, and they were experienced. They could haul the weight.

The Fourth Watch

I WAS REVIVED from my zombie tank on 30 September, eight months and twenty days after the *Medical Explorer's* departure from the Moon.

Awakening from coma-like biostasis was by no means pleasant; it felt very much like being resurrected from the grave. Dr Tanaka would not allow me out of my bed in Deck 2-F, the ship's hibernation bay, until he was convinced that I was ready to walk on my own, even in the one-tenth gravity of Arm Two. Through an archway on the other side of the deck, I could see a sealed zombie tank which contained one of the ship's two other passengers: Marianne Tillis, a ConSpace administrator who, I was told, was scheduled to make an inspection of Valhalla Station.

Tillis wasn't scheduled to be revived until we had arrived at Callisto. On the other hand, Dr Karl Hess, a German astrogeologist, had been resuscitated two months earlier when the *Medici Explorer* had passed Halley's comet in the asteroid belt. Hess was a heavyset man with a pale moustache and a prematurely balding head. He came once to visit me briefly while I was recuperating; although polite, he seemed very nervous, leaving as soon as Yoshio reappeared. Hess spent the remainder of the trip in the passenger deck in Arm One, taking his meals alone in the galley.

Yoshio later told the reason why he had become a hermit. Three weeks earlier, he had cornered his first-wife, Leslie, in the hydroponics bay and had made a rather insistent pass at her, and was only deterred when Old Bill happened to stop by. There had been no violence, but the captain had warned him to keep away from Leslie Smith-Tanaka. By then, Hess already had seemed to realize that he was now *persona non grata* aboard the *Medici Explorer*.

'It happens now and then,' Yoshio said. 'Occasionally, you meet someone who thinks that extended marriage means anything goes.

They believe that if a woman can sleep with three different men, then it won't matter if she has a fourth partner for a little while.' He shrugged off-handedly. 'I've become used to it. I don't even hold a grudge against Dr Hess. . . . just so long as he doesn't come near Leslie again.'

The ship was now twenty million kilometres from Jupiter, which seemed a long distance until the first time I spotted the giant planet gliding past one of the hibernation deck windows. Jupiter looked much as it does when observed through an observatory telescope on Earth: a bright, ruddy sphere, its reddish-orange bands distinctly visible, the Red Spot an oval blur in the southern hemisphere. Yet this was not a magnified view, but what I could see with the naked eye, just outside the square window near my bed. To be able to see something that far away so clearly brought home to me the enormity of the planet, and made me only more eager to get out of bed, no matter how weak I felt.

Yoshio was a good host. He brought me the few messages I had received from home before Earth had gone around the far side of the Sun, severing communications between the ship and the deep-space network based at Descartes City, and helped me with basic callisthenics which gradually restored my muscles. He also sent Wendy Smith-Makepeace to cut my hair, trim my fingernails and toenails, and give me a shave.

Wendy had changed a bit during my long nap. She had celebrated her ninth birthday on 28 July; by coincidence, this was the same day that the ship had made its closest approach to Halley's comet, while the *Medici Explorer* was cruising through the asteroid belt and the comet was heading the other way. While she clipped my hair, Wendy told me about how Cousin Bill let her sit in his lap in one of the observation blisters and study the comet through a telescope; then she had gone down to the wardroom where her mother and Aunt Lynn had baked her a special birthday cake (sans candles, of course – no inflammables were allowed aboard ship). Wendy looked a little taller, and she wasn't quite as solemn as she had been when I had first met her; when I told her a little joke about a twentieth-century rock band called Bill Haley and the Comets, she laughed gaily, beaming a smile which made me realize that, ten years from now, she would be a true heartbreaker.

She was also a good barber and manicurist; once she was through, I looked pretty much as I had before I climbed into the tank. Yet when I told her so, her small face tightened up again. 'I'm only doing this because I practice on my uncles and Captain Montrose,' she said reproachfully. 'I don't want to be a barber . . . Aunt Lynn is trading me to be a hydroponicist!' Then she climbed down off the stool behind me, laid down her scissors, and stiffly walked out of the hibernation bay, leaving me with the impression that I had insulted her intelligence.

Saul Montrose came to visit me at the end of my convalescence. It was the first time we had met since our brief introduction in ConSpace's Descartes City offices, just before the *Medici Explorer* had departed from the Moon. During the past eight months he had shaved off most of his beard, retaining long sideburns and a handlebar moustache which lent his face a rather Victorian appearance.

Saul seemed pleased to have me awake; he sat on the edge of the bed and gave me a quick rundown of the major events of the outbound trip. There was not much to tell: a midflight course correction on 11 April, just before the ship had entered the asteroid belt, which had taken the *Medici Explorer* slightly out of the plane of the elliptic, and the close encounter with Halley's on 28 July, during which he, Dr Hess and Young Bill had conducted extensive long-range scans of the comet's core and corona.

Four days ago, the *Medici Explorer* had navigated the first marker of the Jovian system, when it had passed through the so-called 'bow shock' caused by the collision of the solar wind with Jupiter's magnetosphere ('We hardly felt a tremble,' Saul says). Only yesterday the ship had crossed the orbit of the outmost moon, Sinope, located almost 24 million kilometres from Jupiter. While the ship traversed the orbits of the remaining three moons in the system's outer belt – Pasiphae, Carme, and Ananke – its crew had performed the critical rollover manoeuvre, during which the *Medici Explorer* and its drones had been rotated 180 degrees on their lateral axes until their main engines were facing Jupiter. Once all four vessels were flying backward, the first of several engine burns had been executed, slowing the convoy against the tug of Jupiter's gravity.

Everything else was minor. Geoffrey Smith-Makepeace had

broken his right thumb while fixing a broken internal hatch in Arm One, but it was healed now. Old Bill had been forced to go EVA to repair a frozen valve in one of the aft manoeuvring engines, and he was still struggling to keep it from gimballing incorrectly. Leslie and Lynn had lost a rack of tomatoes in the hydroponics deck when Wendy had failed to set the timer on the UV lamps for a few days.

Other than that, there was nothing else to report.

'Nothing else?' I asked, and Saul gave me a blank look. 'The crew is doing OK? There's been no . . . disagreements? Arguments? Fights?'

Saul smiled a little, the corners of his elegant moustache curling upwards. Yoshio, standing nearby, turned away and pretended to examine a cabinet of surgical equipment.

'Sure, there's been disagreements,' Montrose said quietly. 'Kaneko won't eat his greens until Leslie threatens to spank him at the table . . . he says asparagus makes him sick. Betsy wanted to try a new program she's devised for the navigation system but Old Bill wouldn't let her, and since Geoff keeps losing to Leslie in poker he claims she's cheating, but I don't think he's really serious.' He shrugged indifferently. 'Nothing much. Why?'

I wasn't willing to let it go at that. Yoshio had already told me about Hess's pass at Leslie Smith-Tanaka; however minor the incident had been, it was still an indication that not all was well aboard the ship. 'C'mon, skipper,' I said as I sat up in bed. 'You know better than that. You told me yourself that nothing ever goes perfect on any long voyage. Now you're telling me that this has been a perfect trip so far . . .'

I let the unspoken question hang in the air. Yoshio coughed into his fist and excused himself from the room, the soles of his stikshoes whisking softly on the carpet as he walked through the archway to the other side of the hibernation bay. Saul watched him leave before he turned back to me. 'Mr Cole . . . Elliot . . . how well do you know my record?'

He knew perfectly well that he was the only crewmember I had interviewed before boarding the *Medici Explorer*. Saul Montrose had spent a considerable part of his life working in space, much of it as the first mate, then as captain, aboard the Skycorp cycleship *Percival Lowell*. When ConSpace had offered him the job of commanding the *Medici Explorer* for this run to the Jovian system, he had taken the assignment even though it was a one-shot deal.

Although the Smiths are permanent crewmembers, ConSpace replaces the *Medici Explorer*'s captain after each voyage. One reason is that ConSpace has more deep-space captains than it does spacecraft; in order to keep all the commanders employed, the Spacers Union has mandated that captains be rotated once every two years. The other reason is that, at least in theory, having a new commander once each voyage would keep the crew on its toes, whereas a permanent captain would inevitably allow the crew to fall into familiar, lazy patterns.

Montrose is the one crewmember of the *Medici Explorer* who is not part of the Smith clan. In fact, since he is expressly forbidden by company regulations from becoming involved with any member of the clan, he cannot marry into the extended family. Long-term hormone suppressants injected into his bloodstream before launch guarantee that his sexual urges are kept safely in check for the duration of the voyage. His role is that of a benevolent tyrant, the final arbiter of personal disagreements and consensus decisions. Even if, in the most extreme instance, the Smiths were to mutiny against him, he alone holds the trump card: the ship's master computer will not obey any major set of commands unless his retina scan confirms his presence on the bridge.

'You have to believe me when I tell you,' Saul continued, 'that this crew is as close to perfect as any captain can expect. Sure, there's bickering and arguments. Yoshio gets mad at Old Bill, and he gets pissed off at Leslie, and she has a falling out with Betsy, and Betsy takes it out on Geoff. Same with the kids . . . Young Bill's not really talking to Kaneko right now, and when they get into fights over something, Wendy usually steps in for Kaneko 'cause he's the youngest.'

He shrugged again. 'So what? Families do that. They have little spats and feuds and rivalries, but it doesn't stop them from being a family.' He grinned a little, patting the covers of my bed. 'Lemme tell you something, though . . . when I ran the *Lowell* a few years ago, I once had to throw a guy on the floor and sedate him because he was threatening to push a crewmate into the airlock and punch the button . . . and he meant it, too. You know why? He snored in his sleep.'

'And you haven't seen anything like that?' I asked.

'Not a bit.'

His reply came candidly, with absolute certainty, but even then, I wasn't willing to trust him entirely. It sounded just a little too utopian. I didn't think Saul Montrose was lying – his omission of the Hess incident could be excused as tact, considering we were within Yoshio's earshot – but I wasn't about to buy his version of events as objective truth.

I said nothing, though, only folded my hands together on my chest and waited for him to go on. We gazed at each other for a few moments before he spoke up again. 'You don't believe me, do you?' he asked.

'I didn't say that,' I replied. 'I'm only waiting for you to prove it to me.'

Saul smiled . . . and then he suddenly swatted my left knee with the flat of his right hand. I flinched a little, and he grinned broadly. 'Reflexes look good. Can you lift that leg?'

I raised it beneath the bedcovers and wiggled my foot for good measure. He nodded again, then pulled a pen out of his vest pocket. 'Catch,' he said, then tossed it to me. I grabbed for the pen; Coriolis effect caused by the rotation of the ship's arms almost caused me to miss it, but I managed to clumsily snag the pen from midair.

'Good deal.' Saul took the pen from my hand, then stood up from the bed. 'And you're able to walk OK?'

I demonstrated by throwing off the covers, swinging my legs off the bed, and walking a few steps. I couldn't wait to get out of the hibernation bay; I would have done handsprings if he had requested it. Although it was close to midnight by ship time, all I really wanted to do was walk around the vessel a little before making my way to my quarters in Arm One.

The captain, though, had other plans for me. 'Very good,' he said. 'I'll tell Yoshio you're fit for duty immediately.'

'Pardon me?' I shook my head, wondering if Montrose was kidding. If he wasn't, then the *Medici Explorer* had to be the first ship where the passengers were pressed into duty.

Saul seemed to read my mind. He nodded his head slowly, confirming that I am, indeed, expected to work while I'm aboard his vessel. 'Nothing you won't be able to handle, of course,' he said, 'but we're coming up on the fourth watch and we could use someone else to keep an eye on things in the bridge . . . I can't stay awake all the time, y'know.'

He stepped toward the hatch leading to the access shaft. 'When you're dressed, report at once to the bridge. Twenty-four hundred, sharp. Young Bill and Betsy will be standing watch with you until oh-six-hundred. They'll brief you on what you'll need to do for them. Yoshio . . .? I believe Mr Cole's ready to leave now.'

Then, without waiting for a response from the physician, he was out the hatch and climbing up the ladder toward the ship's hub. I turned to Yoshio, ready to plead my case, but Smith-Tanaka was already extending a stack of neatly folded clothing to me; after a second, I recognized the trousers, shirt and pullover as my own clothes, last seen nine months ago when I brought them aboard the *Medici Explorer* in my duffel bag.

'I took the liberty of fetching these from your quarters,' he said with just a trace of a smile as I took them from his arms. 'There was . . . ah, a certain possibility that the skipper might ask you stand watch as soon as you were able.'

With no possibility of a medical deferment, all I could do was nod my own head as I pulled off the one-piece gown I had been wearing for the past two days. Again, it became blatantly obvious: aboard the *Medici Explorer*, everyone was expected to pull their own weight.

Twenty minutes later, I had managed to climb the long ladder up the Arm Two shaft, negotiate the rotating hatches of the hub carousel, and make my way up the second ladder to the bridge.

Although there is no natural night or day in deep space, the pattern is subtly replicated aboard the *Medici Explorer*. Lights are automatically dimmed through the vessel, major systems are put on automatic, and most of the crew goes to sleep. I have heard of space vessels where the nocturnal sounds of crickets, rain, and summer breezes are piped through the corridors and compartments, but the artificial night was not taken that far aboard the *Medici Explorer*. It would have been absurd to hear bullfrogs croaking aboard a spacecraft hundreds of millions of kilometres from the nearest swamp.

Yet there was a subtle peace of a different kind: the low, almost inaudible throb of the nuclear engines, the vacant shaftway which echoed with each footfall on the ladder rung, the closed hatches and the subdued half-light of recessed fluorescent tubes. Instead of crickets or bullfrogs, one of the AIs – Ditz, probably, or maybe its twin Jethro – scaled the walls of the Arm Two shaft, endlessly prowling for lint and trash. The peace of a deep-space vessel, cruising through the outer reaches of the solar system.

Besides the number of ladder rungs I had to conquer, it took me three attempts before I figured out how to duck through the carousel hatches without bashing my head against a bulkhead . . . and I had to make the transition from one-tenth gravity to the microgravitational environment of the hub without losing my dinner. Fortunately, my nausea passed before I pushed open the top hatch of the hub shaft and glided, albeit clumsily, into the command centre.

The ceiling fluorescents had been lowered to an almost twilight level; the sharpest glow came from the myriad red, green, blue and silver displays from the vacant duty stations. Most of the holoscreens had been switched off, but on the ones which were still active, distant Jupiter shined like the beacon of a faraway lighthouse on a midnight sea. Some of the flatscreens displayed rotating, three-dimensional images of the planet's rings, its plasma torus, the vast curving network of its vast electromagnetic fields, and the orbits of its sixteen moons. Yet Jupiter itself dominated even the most complex of these computer-enhanced images, as if the giant planet was the sun it could have once been, dominating a miniature solar system.

I found Young Bill and Betsy Smith-Makepeace in the alcove on the other side of the bridge, seated next to each other and drinking coffee from squeezebulbs. Young Bill looked no different than when I first met him nine months earlier; he watched with open amusement as I slowly made my way across the bowl-shaped compartment, carefully placing the soles of my stikshoes against the carpet, step by tentative step, my arms thrown out for balance as if I was walking a tightrope.

'Hey, reporter!' he called out as I passed the captain's chair in the centre of the deck. 'You want some coffee?'

'Yeah,' I replied, still watching my feet. 'Love some.'

'Ok . . . catch!' He unhooked another squeezebulb from the coffee dispenser on the shelf behind them and, before I could do more than squawk, tossed it toward me.

'Bill!' Betsy yelled. 'That's cruel!' As I flailed helplessly for the squeezebulb, tumbling end over end toward me, the young woman unsnapped her seat belt and used her arms to push herself out of her chair.

Her grace was as phenomenal as her trajectory was unerring; she glided to the ceiling of the bridge, pushed off again with her hands, performed a midair somersault which tucked her legs behind her body, hurtled down toward me and managed to intercept the squeezebulb before it could hit me.

Grasping the back of the centre chair with her left hand, the navigator handed the coffee to me, smiling sweetly. 'Hi, I'm Betsy. We've met before, haven't we?'

' 'Aw, c'mon!' Bill protested. 'I introduced you two before we launched!'

She cast a sour look over her shoulder at him. 'That's Bill. He's a jerk.' Turning to me again, her smile reappeared. 'You should try not using those shoes so much,' she said, glancing at my feet. 'You look like a baby, doing it that way. Trust me, you don't need your legs to move around in here. I never did.'

'Yeah,' said Young Bill, 'but your legs aren't worth . . .'

'Hush!' Betsy snapped, again glaring reproachfully at him. This time, though, there was a hint of real anger in her voice. Bill shut up and stayed shut-up; his face reddened and he looked away, visibly embarrassed.

Betsy returned her attention to me. 'All you really need to do,' she continued, 'is figure out a straight line to where you want to go, then gently push yourself toward it. If it's a big area, then aim for short distances along the way . . . like this.'

She pushed off the wingback chair, glided to a handrail on a nearby bulkhead and rebounded off that to the chair in front of the engineering station, finally braking herself with her hands in front of the alcove where Young Bill was seated. As she did so, I noticed something unusual; at no time did she use her legs. It was all done with her hands and arms.

Nor did her legs seem quite right. Although at first glance they appeared to be normally developed, I now noticed that they seemed to be perpetually bent at the knees and hips, as if the joints had been locked into a sitting position.

It suddenly dawned on me that this woman, however athletic she might be in zero-gee, could not walk in Earth-normal gravity.

'OK.' Betsy said once she had retaken her seat in the alcove. 'Your turn.'

I tucked the squeezebulb into a pocket of my pullover, then unstuck my shoes and carefully pushed away from the captain's station, following her course toward the alcove. My first real effort in moving through microgravity was neither as accurate nor as liquid as Betsy's – while trying to emulate her smooth bounce off Old Bill's chair, I missed the target and came too close to slamming into his console – but I finally managed my way to the empty seat in the rest area.

I fished the squeezebulb out of my pocket and held it up; through all of this, it had remained unbroken. A small victory. Betsy beamed at me and clapped her hands. Young Bill grinned, nodding his head approvingly. I tried to make a low bow and almost plummeted head-first into the chair.

'Whoa!' Bill shouted, reaching up to stop me. 'Don't run before you can walk.'

'Right. I'll try to remember that.' I hauled myself into the chair, buckled the seat belt, and took a long sip through the straw. The coffee had turned lukewarm by now, but I was thirsty enough not to care. As I drank, my eyes wandered again toward Betsy's legs. She was wearing aquamarine leggings beneath a long woollen sweater; while she was seated, her legs seen normal enough, but . . .

'Something on your mind, Mr Cole?' she asked. It was not a hostile question, but it was clearly a challenge; she had obviously noted my attention. I looked at her and for the first time I noticed her eyes: bright blue, very sharp and direct, much like her precocious daughter's.

I coughed as cold coffee went down the wrong side of my throat. Betsy waited patiently until I recovered, her gaze never wavering. 'Pardon me,' I said at last. 'I don't mean to be rude, but . . .'

The words faltered in my mouth, but Betsy picks up the rest. 'What's wrong with my legs, you mean,' she said quietly. 'Well, I can't use 'em, to make a long story short.'

She smiled grimly and took another sip from her coffee. 'PPS . . . Post-Polio syndrome. I was one of the Chicago kids.'

Elizabeth Smith-Makepeace was a survivor of the Chicago polio epidemic of the thirties – the Children's Plague, as it was known then, because the first persons infected with the disease had been children under the age of ten.

As the story goes, a polio strain had been introduced into the Chicago school system by a substitute teacher who had unwittingly carried the virus back to the United States after touring North Africa the previous summer. While making his rounds through the city's elementary schools, giving arithmetic and science lessons, the teacher had transmitted the disease to literally hundreds of kids, who in turn passed it on to their friends, parents and relatives.

By the time the Centre for Disease Control in Atlanta had identified the contagion not as influenza – as had been initially diagnosed by most doctors, whose medical training had not included recognizing 'extinct' diseases – but as polio, almost two thousand people in the Great Lakes region had contracted the virus. Quite a few of them died, and many more were permanently disabled, before Chicago was placed under paramilitary quarantine and a mass-immunization programme was put into effect by the CDC.

The majority of the infected children recovered from the plague and were thought to be cured. However, ten to twenty years later, many of the survivors developed Post-Polio syndrome. As Betsy explained it to me, both she and her future husband had been among those who had thought they had conquered polio. Indeed, Geoff Makepeace had by then become a long-distance runner, regularly competing in the New York and Boston marathons when he wasn't studying deep-space communications at Tennessee Tech, while Betsy Kesslbaum had often gone Nordic skiing in the Sierras durings breaks from post-grad work at the Stanford University School of Space Science.

'One semester, I was a perfectly fit college girl. Then one day, next semester . . .' She snapped her fingers. 'Boom, I couldn't get out of bed. In a few weeks, I went from cross-country skier to wheelchair jockey.' She shrugged, solemn but without a trace of self-pity. 'Life's a bitch like that sometimes.'

The only good thing about contracting PPS was that she met Geoff while undergoing therapy at the Warm Springs Rehabilitation Institute, although they had both – ironically enough – grown up only a few blocks apart from each other in the same North Chicago neighbourhood. One of the things which brought them together was their shared love of space; when they were married two years later, it was in a public ceremony at the Chicago Museum of Science, in front of the Chesley Bonestell mural of the lunar landscape. The bride wore a white gown inherited from her mother, the groom a black tuxedo from Brooks Brothers. Like at least half of the wedding party, they were both confined to electric carts.

'We knew we wanted to go into space,' Betsy said sixteen years later, sitting in the command centre of a ship bound for Jupiter. 'It wasn't just that we loved the idea and were trained for it. We also knew that, out here, being handicapped doesn't matter as much as it did back on Earth. I mean, let's face it . . . you can be a double-amputee and still function in zero-gee.'

'So you managed to get jobs on this ship,' I said. 'Good idea.'

She shrugged, wadding up her empty squeezebulb and shoving it into the recycle chute behind her. Young Bill pushed himself over to the captain's station, where he entered the mandatory hourly report into the ship's log. As it turned out, there wasn't much expected of the fourth watch except for us to keep each other awake; I suspected that Saul Montrose had assigned me to this job only because Betsy was on the duty roster and he wanted me to meet her.

'It wasn't that easy,' she went on. 'There's a lot of stigma attached to handicapped people . . .' Betsy's mouth twisted into a wry smile. 'Excuse me. "Differently abled persons", since that's the accepted parlance these days . . .'

'Cripples,' I said.

She frowned and wagged a finger at me. 'Now, that really is offensive. If a pro golfer can be handicapped, so can I, but I'll be damned if I'm going to be called a cripple . . . anyway, there's still a lot of stigma attached to disabled persons. Especially in this profession, since the dominant paradigm seems to be that of the rough, tough space hero . . .'

'Captain Future to the rescue,' Bill muttered, his fingers tapping the keypad of his console. 'Two-fisted conquerer of the galaxy, hero of the spaceways. . .'

'Able to drop-kick swarthy aliens over the goal-post of the universe,' Betsy finished. It sounded like an old joke between them. 'If it wasn't for the equal-opportunity clause of the union contracts, Geoff and I would still be riders back in Chicago.'

37

She swivelled around in her chair to pump some more coffee from the urn into a fresh squeezebulb. 'Even then, it was a long time before we were able to get a shot at any deep-space jobs. We lived on the Moon for six years . . . I co-piloted a tug for the Pax while Geoff jockeyed a console in the city . . . and we both had to put up with a lot of crap.'

'Such as?'

She passed the squeezebulb to me and began to fill one for herself. 'For one thing, the Pax was reluctant to let us have Wendy. They thought we might pass the disease on to her, although that's practically impossible since the offspring of polio survivors are usually born immune. The government didn't want to have to support . . . y'know, another cripple. Or worse yet, a kid who could infect the rest of Descartes City with polio.'

'I didn't think polio could be transmitted that way,' I said.

'It can't. That's the whole point. Someone in government was being stupid, thinking polio is a hereditary disease.' Betsy pinched off the squeezebulb lip from the urn, slipped a valve around the nipple, and took a sip. Having finished making his log entry, Bill glided back to the alcove, where he buckled himself into the vacant chair and filled a bulb for himself. 'It took us a long time for the Pax to issue us a pregnancy permit,' she went on, 'and only after we managed to get four different specialists to confirm that Wendy would be born normal would they allow us to go ahead with the pregnancy.'

Betsy winced at the recollection. 'You know, there's almost two hundred children on the Moon now, and a lot of 'em are dumb as a stump . . . believe me, I've met 'em. Spoiled brats. And then you get my child, whom we've had to get the ship's tutorial system to graduate to high school level before she's ten . . . and some morons didn't want her to be born because Geoff and I were Chicago kids.'

'She's very smart.'

Betsy glanced sharply at me, picking up the guarded tone in my voice. 'Yeah,' she said, 'I know she's a pain in the ass sometimes. Sometimes pretty arrogant, too. Last night at dinner she told everyone at the table about cutting your hair yesterday, and then she said, "I thought writers were supposed to be intelligent." '

Young Bill hid his face within his hands, trying to disguise his hysterics as a coughing fit. Betsy simply looked at me with a well-worn look of sympathy. 'Please don't strangle her,' she said, smiling benignly. 'She's only nine.'

'I can show you where the emergency airlocks are located.' Bill managed to gasp. 'One little shove . . .'

'No thanks.' I was tempted to ask permission to turn her over my knee instead; since I was a guest on the ship, though, that might not have been a proper request. Yet it did raise another question . . . 'How is it, raising a kid on a spacecraft? It's not a normal sort of childhood.'

Betsy shrugged offhandedly. 'For her, it's normal,' she said easily. 'Wendy was born on the Moon, after all. She's never been to Earth, so . . .'

'Never?'

Her mother shook her head. 'And probably won't, at least not for a few more years. Of course, Wendy wants to visit Earth. Now that she's decided to be a hydroponicist when she grows up . . . Lynn got her into that . . . she really wants to see what a real, natural garden looks like. But it's going to take a while before she can go. She's in pretty good physical shape, especially for the offspring of two polio survivors, but she will need extensive conditioning before her muscles can take the higher gravity.'

'Ditto for all the inoculations she'll have to receive.' Young Bill said, pulling his mouth away from the straw of his squeezebulb. A tiny brown sphere of coffee leaked from the bulb; he smacked it out of midair with his left hand and absently wiped his palm across an armrest. 'Compared to the biospheres where she's been raised, Earth is like crawling into our septic tank. It takes a while for the body's immunal system to cope. When I was ten years old and went down for the first time, I was sick for the first two weeks, just from breathing the air.'

Betsy nodded. 'She's also going to have to get used to a lot of social differences between spacers and Earth-folk . . . like for instance, the fact that extended families are scarce down there, so an "uncle" or "aunt" to someone else is not the same as one of her own uncles or aunts.' She smiled coyly. 'So it's not nice to ask someone if their mother is sleeping with their uncle.'

That remark raised yet another question. 'ConSpace received a lot of negative publicity when it chose to put extended familes on the Jupiter run. The Christian Defense League, for instance, has called upon clergymen to issue a blanket condemnation of ConSpace and its shareholders. How do you feel about that?'

Betsy and Bill shared a sour look; Bill coughed into his fist while Betsy heaved a great sigh. ' "How do you feel about that?" ' Bill repeated. 'Like I really give a royal shit what a bunch of fanatics say about . . .'

'Bill.' Betsy's voice is soft yet admonishing. Young Bill shut up, looking away from us both and muttering under his breath.

Betsy looked at me again. 'For one thing,' she said, 'the CDL didn't say anything about the extended families which have been on the Moon and Clarke County for the past thirty years. Even though Geoff and I aren't particularly religious and neither are Leslie or Yoshio, Lynn and Old Bill are devout Mormons. Their church came around almost ten years ago, and that's one of the strictest Christian sects. So bringing up the issue now is a little late, don't you think?'

'None the less . . .'

'None the less, the issue has been raised.' Betsy sighed again and folded her hands together in her lap. 'Look, the gist of it is that the CDL believes that we're living in a state of sin, that we're teaching our children about sexual promiscuity, blah blah and so forth. My response . . . if I'm even going to stoop to making a response to Reverend Haynes and his followers . . . is that these are a bunch of dirty-minded people prying into my private business, and that how we raise our kids is our own affair. Period.'

Young Bill seemed anxious to put in his opinion; I only had to glance toward him for the teenager to eagerly jump in. 'I can't believe some of the things I've read about us,' he said heatedly. 'These yahoos seem to think that we're all out here having mass orgies, banging each others brains out, parents molesting their kids, all that shit.' He laughed, but with scarcely any humour. 'If that were true, I wouldn't still be a virgin, for Christ's sakes!'

Betsy's face turned bright red, but she said nothing. If his parents were devout Mormons, their beliefs obviously hadn't affected their first-son very much. 'Aunt Betsy's right,' he went on. 'It ain't nobody's business but ours . . . but if I could get my hands on Haynes and his crew, I'd . . .'

'Bill . . .' his aunt said again.

He held up his hands. 'OK, OK.' He took a deep breath, getting his temper back under control. 'But do you see what it's like, growing up in an environment like this? If it weren't for the fact that this is my family, I'd . . .'

It was at that moment when the reflective calm of the fourth watch was shattered.

A sharp electronic buzz from across the command centre jerked the conversation to an abrupt halt. For an instant, both crewmen froze in their seats . . .

'Ah, shit,' Young Bill murmured as he fumbled for the release catch of his seat belt. Betsy had already unsnapped her own belt and launched herself out of her chair. She quickly manoeuvred along ceiling rungs until she reached the communications station on the opposite side of the bridge. Her speed was phenomenal; before Bill made his way across the deck and I clumsily followed them both, Betsy had strapped herself into Geoff's chair and had pulled a headset over her ears.

'Jupiter station, this is one-twelve Whisky Bravo Nebraska,' she said tersely, her fingers moving quickly across the keypad in front of her as she typed in a set of commands. 'Jupiter station, this is one-twelve Whisky Bravo Nebraska, DSV *Medici Explorer*. Do you copy? Please identify yourself, over.'

Young Bill reached the com station and held on to the back of the chair, staring over Betsy's shoulder at the computer displays. 'That's the computer's signal for an SOS,' he said quietly to me. 'Can't be from anywhere else except somewhere in Jupiter space.'

It takes almost an hour for a radio transmission from the inner planets to reach the Jovian system. By then, whatever emergency might have taken place on Earth, the Moon, or Mars, would have already passed, even if the *Medici Explorer* had been close enough to render assistance. None the less, the ship was just within the outer belt of Jovian moons; getting a strong fix on the signal through Jupiter's electromagnetic fuzz and clatter was like trying to locate the source of a fleeting searchlight in the midst of a dense ocean fog.

Betsy listened intently to the carrier-wave static, repeating the ship's call-sign over and over as she scanned the radio bands. Ten minutes passed before she succeeded in getting a clear fix on the incoming signal and locked on with the transceiver. 'We copy, four-fifteen Delta Tango Romeo,' she said. 'This is one-twelve

Whisky Brave Nebraska, *Medici Explorer* . . . Please repeat your message, over.'

Again, she listened closely. Although her face remained calm, her eyes widened slightly as I overheard a tinny, indistinct voice through her headset. 'We copy and confirm, four-fifteen Delta Tango Romeo,' she said at last. 'Please relay your co-ordinates and we'll assist. Over.'

She pushed aside the right cup of her headset and looked up at Young Bill. 'Better wake up your dad, Uncle Geoff, Uncle Yoshio, and the skipper,' she said. 'A boat from Valhalla Station has gone down on Amalthea. One dead, one wounded, and one on the rocks.' She shook her head as she refastened her headset to her ear. 'Looks like we might to have to send someone in. Damn.'

'I'm on it.' Bill peered more closely over her shoulder at the computer screen, his lips moving silently as he quickly committed a series of numbers to memory, before he vaulted toward the captain's station.

'If you were hoping for a boring story,' he said to me in midflight, 'you've come to the wrong place.'

Fathers And Mothers

B Y THE TIME fourth watch ended, most of the crew was already awake and had been summoned to the bridge where Betsy and Young Bill had continually monitored the emergency on Amalthea. Wendy Smith-Makepeace, sleepy-eyed but none the less eager to help, was sent to the galley on Deck 1-F to fetch an early breakfast; she returned carrying a bag of hot English muffins and dried fruit, which the adults consumed while sitting at their consoles. There was no time this morning for a sit-down meal in the wardroom.

Although there was very little I could do besides make coffee and refill squeezebulbs, no one objected to my presence on the bridge, although William Smith-Tate was clearly unhappy about my hanging around the command centre. Although he didn't say anything to me, his chill demeanour expressed his unspoken opinion that the bridge was no place for passengers during an emergency, especially not when they're journalists. However, the fact that Saul Montrose hadn't thrown me out of the command centre was a clear demonstration that he wanted to have me around; he was the captain, after all, and his word was law. 'If you're going to write about what we do,' Saul told me during a slow moment, 'you might as well see what it's like when we've got a crisis situation.'

And the situation was critical indeed. Once Geoff took over the com station from his wife, he eventually gleaned further details through garbled communications with both the downed ship on Amalthea and, later, Callisto Station. Four-one-five DTR was the radio call-sign for the JSS *Barnard,* a short-range shuttle that flew sorties within the Jovian system; it had crashed on Amalthea while attempting take-off from the tiny moon. There were three persons aboard the *Barnard:* pilot Wayne Reese, co-pilot Marlon

Bellafonte and an engineer, Casey Nimersheim. Reese had been killed immediately and Bellafonte has suffered massive internal injuries, leaving Nimersheim the only person capable of talking to anyone. She had done well to patch things together as best she could, but the audible quaver in her voice showed she was frightened by what had happened and confused about what to do next.

Amalthea is the third-inmost of Jupiter's satellites, a potato-shaped rock only 280 kilometres in length, located scarcely 181,000 klicks from the planet. Amalthea's period and close proximity to Jupiter makes it an excellent site for an automatic relay station between the floating *Prometheus 1* helium-3 factory and Callisto Station; since the moon orbits its primary once every twelve hours, it's almost perpetually above *Prometheus 1*, allowing controllers on Callisto to maintain near-continuous telemetry with the Jovian atmospheric factory.

A tiny, unmanned installation had been placed within Pan Crater on Amalthea. It was serviced by several AIs, and under normal circumstances operated smoothly, but there were frequent breakdowns, usually caused by deterioration of electronic components by intense radiation. Amalthea is buried deep within Jupiter's harsh magnetosphere and plasma torus; as such it is located within one of the most hostile zones in the solar system, and because of this the automated outpost was prone to malfunctions.

In this instance (we were finally told by Callisto Station, which seemed to have trouble getting someone knowledgeable on-line) three of Pan Base's six computers had suffered concurrent hardware failures that could not be easily fixed by the robots. Callisto Station had been forced to send a repair mission down to Amalthea so that Nimersheim could replace vital modules in the three stricken computers. The mission had gone well; the engineer successfully made the repairs . . . but then, as the *Barnard* was attempting to lift off from Pan Base, something had gone wrong during launch that caused the shuttle not to achieve escape velocity. Instead, it had lost altitude and crashed bow-first into the crater wall.

The pilot was killed instantly when the fuselage of the cockpit module caved in on impact. The co-pilot was critically injured and was now in shock and unconscious; it was only because

Nimersheim was in the rear passenger seat that she escaped harm. Although the cockpit's atmospheric integrity had been breached, all three persons were wearing hardsuits during take-off, and Nimersheim reported that she had patched oxygen lines between Bellafonte's suit and her own into the *Barnard's* central life-support system. Air supply was not an immediate problem, nor was radiation exposure – the shuttle had a 72-hour emergency reserve, and the craft's radiation shields had not been breached – but Bellafonte's injuries made their swift rescue a high priority.

Because Amalthea had been on Jupiter's solar nearside when the distress signal was sent from the *Barnard,* and Callisto's orbit was on the far side, the *Medici Explorer* had been the first radio receiver to pick up Casey Nimersheim's mayday. There are two other relay stations on Io and Europa, but bouncing transmissions between four moons and the *Medici Exporer* still took considerable effort, much like playing billiards on a table whose pockets are in constant motion. It was almost two hours before Geoff and Saul could establish a reliable three-way line of communication between Callisto, Amalthea and the *Medici Explorer.*

During this time, Yoshio conversed with Nimersheim on one channel, calming down the panicky scientist and talking her through in-suit first-aid procedures for Bellafonte. Meanwhile, on another channel, Old Bill was in continual communication with two controllers at Callisto Station, trying to get an accurate assessment of their situation while simultaneously working with Betsy to run complex orbital-mechanics problems through the bridge computers. Leslie used Nimersheim's blurry, disjointed descriptions of the *Barnard*'s internal condition in an attempt to gauge the full extent of the damage suffered and, most importantly, judge how much longer the ship's emergency life-support system would hold up. Young Bill temporarily assumed the captain's chair where he monitored the *Medici Explorer*'s vital signs, while Saul himself struggled to co-ordinate everything at once.

Everyone was simultaneously talking. Three-dimensional displays appeared and vanished from computer screens with bewildering swiftness; data was input, output and considered, with alternatives quickly accepted or rejected. The scene resembled the ship's launch from lunar orbit eight months earlier, except this time the stakes were much higher: the lives of two people hung upon minute-by-minute decisions.

It became apparent that Callisto Station was expecting the *Medici Explorer* to perform the rescue mission almost single-handedly, as if the lucky accident of having received the first SOS from the *Barnard* had shifted the responsibility for the rescue operation upon the crew of the incoming vessel. Instead of arguing with Callisto, though, the crew had decided, without any real discussion, to take the weight upon their own shoulders.

While Betsy, Saul and Old Bill hashed out the details of a rescue mission, I wandered over to the captain's station, where Young Bill was running a diagnostics check on the main computer bus. 'I don't get it,' I said, pointing to a flatscreen halo chart of the Jovian system. 'We're nearly ten million kilometres from Amalthea, but Callisto is only about two million klicks away. Why can't they rescue their own people?'

The kid didn't look up from his work. 'Believe me,' Young Bill said softly, 'if you were stranded down there and had a choice between us or them to save your ass, you'd rather have us. Chances are the shuttle went down because some idiot wasn't maintaining the engines properly . . . and if that's the case, there's no guarantee the other boats aren't screwed up the same way.'

'You're kidding.'

Bill shook his head. 'You'll see what I mean when we get there. The whole base is held together with duct tape and solder.' He glanced over his shoulder, to see if anyone overheard our discussion. 'We might be farther out,' he whispered, 'but we're the best chance those poor suckers have. We know it and Callisto knows it, even if they won't come right out and admit it.'

He hesitated. 'Besides, my dad wouldn't have it any other way. He's had to do this kind of thing before.'

Before I could ask what he meant, Young Bill returned his attention to his job, hunching over the keyboard as he concentrated on the diagnostic chart.

For once, the kid didn't want to talk, and I was too tired to question him further. My eyelids were beginning to feel gritty; it had been many hours since I last slept, and despite the circumstances, I realized that it would still be many hours before the rescue operation got underway. Noticing my exhaustion, Saul relieved me from duty. 'Go below and get some winks,' he said. 'I'll call you when things change.'

I didn't argue with his orders. I left the bridge and made my way through the ship to the passenger quarters in Arm One. It was the first time I had seen my cubicle since *Medici Explorer* was in orbit above the Moon. I didn't even bother to undress before I dimmed the lights and lay down on the bunk. Yet, even as my weary eyes were closing of their own accord, I caught a last glimpse of Jupiter floating past the window.

The planet was now the apparent size of a soccer ball, its thin ring visible in the weak light of the distant sun. It disappeared from sight, and I fell asleep wondering how Jupiter must look through the shattered cockpit windows of the *Barnard*, crashed on a tiny captured asteroid deep within the planet's lethal radiation belts.

My last waking thoughts were an agnostic's prayer for the frightened young woman marooned on Amalthea.

I slept for only six hours, but it seemed like much longer by the time Betsy chimed my intercom to tell me that the captain was ready to brief me about the rescue mission.

The first thing I noticed upon crawling out of the bunk was that the window had been opaqued by metal shutters; now that the vessel was deeper in-system, the arm windows had been irised shut to lessen radiation exposure. It was my first clue as to how dangerous the mission would be.

After I dressed, I visited the head to brush my teeth and splash some cold water on my face. Showers are only allowed once every three days in order to conserve water, and my last bath was only two days ago, when Yoshio had sponged me down shortly after I had been resuscitated from the zombie tank. Karl Hess, the only other revived passenger aboard ship, was already in the passenger head; unlike myself, he was due for his shower, and I caught him while he was towelling off in the stall. Despite his self-imposed exile, Hess was aware of the emergency on Amalthea, having monitored bridge transmissions through his cabin computer.

'I hope they manage to get those people of that rock,' he said with utter sincerity, yet when I asked him if he wanted to accompany me to the bridge, he declined the invitation: 'The Smiths would probably not appreciate my company.' He made no mention of the sexual overtures he had made towards Leslie Smith-Tanaka, nor did I press the issue.

On my way up the access shaft, I noticed that the hatch to Deck 1-C was ajar. I stopped on the ladder and peered inside; Wendy and Kaneko are seated on the carpeted floor, absorbed in a game of scissors-cuts-paper. It looked like Wendy was winning. They didn't notice my spying, so I moved on up the ladder, heading for the bridge.

I paused in the foyer to study the holoscreen displays. The ship's position was marked by a blue oval, gliding through the dense silver strands of Jupiter's radiation fields; other screens depicted the orbits of Elara, Lysithea, Himalia and Leda. While I had slept, the *Medici Explorer* had passed deeper into the Jovian system; dead ahead were the orbits of the Galilean satellites. Callisto was a tiny, slate-grey orb, less than a million nautical miles from our present heading, and Ganymede was magnified on one screen as a tiny, brightly spotted replica of Mercury.

Jupiter dominated each real-time camera image; it was an enormous bull's-eye in the centre of every computer simulation. One screen showed a close-up view of the planet; I found myself transfixed by the rotating milky-white and reddish-orange bands of its cloud patterns, each describing their own clockwise movement through the upper stratosphere. As I watched, the Red Spot slowly moved into view from Jupiter's farside, a vast scarlet wound in the southern hemisphere where a hurricane large enough to devour five Earths has raged as long as recorded human history and perhaps much longer.

Magnificent swirl and ebb, flux and flow. The bridge was much quieter now. Young Bill was absent, having finally been relieved from duty, but Betsy was still holding her post at the navigation board. Wendy cleaned away trays and sandwich wrappers left over from lunch, the second consecutive meal to have been eaten in the command centre. I noticed that William Smith-Tate wasn't around; when I asked Saul why, he told me that Old Bill was checking out the ship's boat for the rescue mission.

As it turned out, the chief engineer would be flying the *Marius* down to Amalthea to pick up the crash survivors. And, unless Yoshio Smith-Tanaka managed to win the argument between the two men, he would be doing it alone.

The captain typed a command into his keyboard, bringing up a schematic diagram on a flatscreen at his station. Although the three cargo freighters would continue on the prearranged trajectory to Callisto, the *Medici Explorer* had already broken away from the convoy and had diverted its heading to fly closer to Jupiter. Two of its four main-engine retrofires had already been cancelled, in order to cut down the number of hours until periapsis, the ship's closest approach to Jupiter.

The mission profile called for *Medici Explorer* to make a polar flyby of Jupiter. In order to avoid the equatorial plasma torus between Io and Jupiter, the vessel would fly beneath the torus, heading towards the planet's south pole. Although the *Explorer* would never get closer than Io's orbit, it would launch the *Marius* once we had passed under the torus.

'Once we get here,' Montrose said as he rotated the diagram to display the far side of Jupiter, 'we'll fire main engines again to put us in a slingshot trajectory up and over Jupe's north pole. That'll get us above the plasma torus again, and Bill can fly up to meet us there. It'll be tricky, but we've run it through the computers a few times and they say we can do it.'

What's tricky about it? 'First, Bill's going to be cutting it close,' Saul explained. 'From beginning to end, he's got about six hours to find the crash site, land safely, transfer the survivors over to his ship, and launch again. Remember now, everyone's going to be wearing exos, so it'll slow them down a bit on the surface.'

The captain tapped a couple more commands into the computer. The simulation shifted to Jupiter's north pole and a long orange-tinted fantail appeared on the screen, sweeping outward from the planet. 'Then we've got to deal with the leeside of the magnetosphere,' he continued. 'The solar wind blows all that radiation outward from the planet, so there's quite a bit of turbulence over there which we just can't avoid. Solar-side, the magnetosphere extends only about eight million kilometres from Jupiter. We can handle that without much problem . . . but on the leeside, it reaches almost out to Saturn. This ship can take it OK, but Bill's going to have to fight his way through it. That, plus having to contend with the gravity well . . .'

He shrugged. 'Well, he can do it, and he wants to do it, so there you go.'

'And he's flying down there by himself?'

The skipper's lips pursed together thoughtfully. 'He says that's the only way he'll do it,' he said slowly. 'The *Marius* can accommodate up to six people, of course, but each person you put aboard adds to the payload mass. The trick isn't so much getting to Amalthea as it is leaving again. He says he needs those few extra litres of fuel to bring the poor bastards home.'

'But you don't agree.'

'Yoshio doesn't. He thinks he needs to go down there to help the wounded man once they've got him off the shuttle, but Bill doesn't want to risk someone else on this mission.' The skipper pointed at another screen; a TV image showed a large, silver-gold spider crawling across the fuselage of the *Marius*. 'That's Tiger, one of the AIs. You haven't met him because he stays outside the ship. Right now he's dismantling every piece of excess mass from the boat, trying to strip it down to its bare essentials . . . right now, see, it's removing a cargo truss.'

Montrose indicated the vertical bar of numbers next to Tiger's image. 'That's Tiger talking to me. When he says that he's shaved the *Marius* down to nothing it can't use, then I'll add up the lost kilos and make the final call. If we lose enough mass for Yoshio to tag along for the ride and still give them a good chance, then I'll override Bill and send the doctor down with him.'

'Have you consulted the company on this?'

Montrose gave me a dour glance. 'We can't communicate with ConSpace,' he said. 'Our current position puts us out of direct radio contact with Earth for another two months. However, I checked it out with the expert-system and it told me the mission isn't out of line with company policy. Everything's been duly entered in the logbook.' He smiled briefly. 'Believe me, I wouldn't do anything drastic without first consulting the company, even if it's only a surrogate decision. If I didn't, our underwriters would shit a brick.'

'And the family? How do they feel about this?'

The captain's smile disappeared. He didn't say anything for a few moments, staring instead at his console screens. I noticed that a chill silence had descended upon the bridge. Although no one was looking at us, the carefully averted eyes of Betsy, Geoff, Leslie and Yoshio told me that they had been listening to the entire

50

conversation. Only Wendy, seated in the rest alcove with her hands properly folded together in her lap, was watching us, her gaze discomfitingly direct.

'It isn't my place to speak for the Smiths.' Montrose said, his tone of voice suddenly cool and formal. 'If you wish to interview one of them, may I suggest that you speak to Bill's first-wife. Lynn's currently on duty in the hydroponics bay, Arm Two.'

Somehow, I had overstepped the boundaries. I murmured an apology, which no one cared to acknowledge, and dismissed myself from the bridge.

The *Medici Explorer*'s hydroponics bay takes up three decks of Arm Two, just above the hibernation area. It's a miniature greenhouse in space, humid and smelling of green, growing things. Patrolling the top deck was Knucklehead, which greeted me less cordially than its brother AI, Ditz: *'Shut the hatch! Wipe your shoes! Don't touch anything!'*

Knucklehead's disposition mirrored that of its mistress. I found Lynn Tate-Smith on the second level, carefully pruning the tomato vines growing from one of the long tanks which are crowded together in the compartment. She barely looked up as I climbed down the ladder.

'I thought you would come to see me sooner or later,' she said. She hesitated, then added, 'It's about my first-husband, isn't it?'

'Yes, ma'am,' I replied as I sat down on a stool placing my notebook on my knees. 'If I could only have a few minutes of your time . . .'

'To ask personal questions so you can fill some more pages of your book.' Her clippers made quick, methodical snips as they moved through the vines, trimming away smaller leaves which she dropped into a pocket of her canvas apron. 'Would you like to know how many interviews I've turned down, Mr Cole? How many other writers have tried to intrude upon my privacy?'

'Your son doesn't have any problems about talking to me,' I said. The clippers paused for a half-second, then continued their work. 'Bill doesn't think I'm an intrusion.'

'My son . . .'. She took a deep breath and carefully placed the clippers down on a table before she turned around. 'My son, if you must know, would rather not be on the ship. In fact, he's all but announced to the family that he wants to leave after this trip. Of course he's willing to talk to you . . . he doesn't think he has anything to lose.'

A quick cynical smile. 'Everything to gain, most likely. He's probably hoping it'll make him a big man at whatever college accepts him on Earth.'

It was the first time I had encountered Lynn Smith-Tate since our brief introduction nine months earlier. She was a tough-looking, no-nonsense woman, whose muscular arms and lean face hinted at a rural heritage. I later learned that her ancestors had been Mormon farmers in Missouri, scrabbling together a liveli-hood while friends and relatives were being torched out of their cabins or hanged by lynch mobs. Like her first-husband, there was very little which seemed lovable, or loving, about her, yet there must have been something hidden beneath her hardbitten exterior which lent itself to intermarriage.

I told her that I didn't think Young Bill was being opportunistic: he was simply being friendly toward a writer whose work he had read and enjoyed. That seemed to reach her; her expression softened a bit as she pulled off her gloves and dropped them on top of the clippers.

'So long as it's short,' she says, 'and it isn't about sex.'

The last thing I wanted to know about this woman was her sexual appetites. 'When I asked your son about his dad flying the rescue mission, he said that he "wouldn't have it any other way". He also said he's done this sort of thing before. What did he mean by that?'

Her eyelids fluttered slightly. 'Why don't you ask him?'

'Because I'm asking you.'

Lynn gazed down at her shoes for a few seconds, then she pushed her hair back and looked straight at me. 'You know about the *Tycho Brahe*, don't you?'

I nodded. 'Bill was the second mate on that mission,' she said. 'He was one of the survivors.'

It had been William Tate, she went on to tell me, who had managed to get the *Brahe* back to Mars, thereby saving the lives of the two other men who had survived the asteroid collision. Because he had done so, he had also been able to rescue his own career. The ISC board of inquiry had ruled him inculpable for the disaster, and one of the reasons ConSpace had chosen the Smith clan was Old Bill's experience aboard the *Brahe*.

'It's haunted him, Mr Cole,' she said. 'No matter what the board ruled, he still believes that he's partially at fault for the *Brahe* disaster . . . even though he wasn't,' she quickly added.

'So that makes him feel responsible for the people down on Amalthea,' I said.

Lynn quickly shook her head. 'No, no, he doesn't think that. He just doesn't want to see anyone else die if he can possibly help it. Since he's the only person who's qualified to fly the *Marius* in a situation like this . . .' Her mouth became a taut, narrow line. 'But it's why he's hard on everyone, even the kids. He's seen what happens when things get loose, and he doesn't want to go through another *Brahe*.'

'So you're not worried about the rescue attempt?'

Again, the faint smile. 'Mr Cole, as far is Bill is concerned, there's no such word as "attempt". You do it once, you do it right, or you don't do it at all. When our son was very young, my husband would spank him if he used an excuse like, "But I tried, Daddy". Maybe that's perfectionism but there's too many people who use such phrases as convenient excuses. Bill won't abide that sort of thinking, and neither will I.'

She shook her head again. 'No, I'm not worried about my Bill. He'll pull off this mission, and he'll come back with the survivors. And that's all there is to it.'

Lynn Smith-Tate picked up her gloves and shoved her calloused hands into them, then took up the clippers again. 'Thanks for not asking me about sex. That was very considerate of you.'

Then she turned back to the tomato vines and recommenced her meticulous pruning. Our conversation was over.

Although there are three decks to the ship's hydroponics bay, one can enter the section only through the hatch at the top level, Deck 2-C; the idea is to contain the humid environment of hydroponics as much as possible. When I climbed up the ladder to 2-C, I discovered that my interview with Lynn Smith-Tate had not been done in privacy.

William Smith-Tate sat on a stool by the hatch. His arms resting on his thighs, his broad shoulders hunched forward, his big hands clasped together between his knees, he resembled a Spanish bull awaiting the arrival of the matador. I didn't ask him if he had been eavesdropping, and he didn't ask me what I had said to his first-wife: the answers to both questions were self-evident, yet he still wanted to know something.

'Are you trying to mess with me?' he said.

I stood beside the ladder, realizing that the confrontation had been inevitable, yet none the less wishing I could disappear in a cloud of vapour. Smith-Tate glowered at me, patiently awaiting my reply, while I wondered whether Yoshio's surgical skills extended as far as being able to reattach my head to the neck.

'No,' I said. 'I'm not trying to mess with you, Bill.'

He stared unblinkingly at me, his hostile gaze never wavering. 'First, you spend a lot of time talking to my boy, wanting to know everything you can about him. That I can maybe understand . . . Bill's an interesting kid. But then you start asking the skipper about me, and when he won't tell you whatever you're trying to find out, you go and talk to my wife. The last person you try to talk to, though, is me. I don't like it when somebody plays games behind my back, Mr Cole.'

'I'm not playing . . .'

'I didn't ask you.' His voice never changed from a dead monotone, yet his anger was all too apparent. He paused as if to collect his thoughts, then he went on. 'Like I said, I don't play games. I'm an honest person, and in return I expect others to be honest with me. I don't like it when I catch people sneaking around behind my back, and that's what you've been doing, Mr Cole.'

'I'm not . . .'

'I'm not finished yet.' Again he paused, this time a little longer, before he continued again. 'So if there's something you want to know about me for your book, then ask me straight. Don't go scurrying around like a stowaway rat with your notebook and recorder, trying to steal little crumbs here and there. Have you got that, Mr Cole?'

There was no point in arguing that he had made himself unapproachable from the moment I crawled through the airlock; the man saw things in only black and white, without any neutral shades. I wondered if he himself was aware of just how daunting he was to normal conversation, let alone journalistic inquiry. In fact, I

suspected that he disregarded my role as a journalist. Like his first-
wife, he saw me as an intruder, and he was the sort of man who
didn't tolerate intrusion.

I slowly nodded my head.

'All right, then,' he said. 'Then here's all you need to know.' He
flicked a hand toward my notebook. 'Go ahead. Take notes if you
want.'

I opened my notebook and switched on the recorder as he held
up a forefinger. 'One. I'm going down there to rescue a couple of
people who need help. It has nothing to do with the *Brahe* . . . that
happened many years ago, and I don't have anything to apologize
for on that score. There's two people on Amalthea who have to be
rescued, and I'm the best man for the job. Period.'

He raised a second finger. 'Two. I'd do it alone if the skipper
would let me. I'm not trying to impress anyone or hog the glory . . .
I'd just rather not risk the lives of anyone else in the family except
my own. Unfortunately, that's not the situation now. We managed
to strip enough junk off *Marius* to allow for another hundred and
forty kilos of payload-mass, and that's just enough to put both
Yoshio and one of the AIs aboard. I have no problem with taking
Tiger with me, but I don't want Yoshio aboard. However, since
that's not my call anymore, so be it.'

'Why are you bringing Tiger?'

'We may need him to cut through the *Barnard*'s hull. Geoff thinks
the airlock hatch may be damaged or buried under rubble, because
the girl down there doesn't see a green light on her status board.
Tiger's laser can do the job quicker than I can, so that's why we're
bringing him.'

Surprisingly, a smile crossed his face. 'You should be happy
about this, Mr Cole. Tiger's outfitted for VR, so you'll be able to
ride him from up here.' His smile faded again. 'Of course, Tiger's
shaped like a spider, but that shouldn't bother you none. You're
probably used to crawling around like a bug.'

I lowered my notebook. 'One more question,' I said, and Old Bill
shrugged. 'What is it that you have against me?'

The engineer stared back at me for a few seconds, then he said,
'Come over here.'

I hesitated, then I crossed the deck to where he sat. 'Put out your
hand,' he said, 'like this.'

He raised his right arm so that it was perpendicular to his body, the palm of his hand hovering rightside-up above the floor.

I did so, imitating his gesture; as I did, he suddenly grabbed my wrist with his left hand, holding it steady, as his right hand dove into the breast pocket of his vest. Before I could react, he pulled out a small alligator clip of the type used for splicing electrical lines . . . then he pinched it on the soft bit of skin at the base of my middle finger.

I yelped and tore my hand out of his grasp. The clip sailed off my palm and landed on the deck beneath his stool. 'Like I thought,' he said, his voice low yet filled with contempt. 'You've got baby's hands. Never done an honest day's work in your life. Haven't held anything tougher than a pen, have you?'

While I sucked at the tiny red bruise left by the clip, Old Bill reached down and picked it up. As I watched, he calmly and effortlessly snagged it to the identical spot within his own hand, turning his palm upside-down and wiggling the clip back and forth to demonstrate the toughness of the callous to which the clip was attached.

'When you can do this,' he said as he unclasped the alligator clip and tossed it at my feet, 'then you can presume to judge me, my family, or anyone else who works out here. Until then, you're just another guy who pushes around words and think they mean something real.'

William Smith-Tate stood up from his stool. 'See you later, Mr Cole,' he murmured. Then, without another word, he opened the hatch and left the deck.

I waited until I was sure he had climbed the Arm Two ladder all the way up to the hub before I took my own leave of the hydroponics bay.

I wanted to shout something after him, but for the first time in many years I didn't know what to say.

Amalthea

ONE MOMENT, THERE was darkness, pitch black and without form or depth, broken only by the sound of my breathing. Then there were pixelated test patterns, like electronic Buddhist sand paintings, flashing against the darkness as Saul's voice spoke in my ears – '*OK, Elliot, here goes*' – and in the next instant I was thrown from one plane of existence and into another.

Suddenly, I was in space, as if I had been jettisoned from the airlock of the *Medici Explorer*. Jupiter loomed before me as an immense sphere that blotted out the stars, streaked by reddish-orange cloud bands which swirled in counter-clockwise harmony, its forbidding nightside a black pit in which tiny flashes of lightning sparked like distant, silent explosions . . .

'*One-twelve Whisky Bravo Nebraska, this is eight-sixteen Victor X-Ray Hotel.*' Old Bill's voice came through my earphones, scratchy and furred with static. '*Downrange ten thousand klicks, bearing X-Ray minus fifty-two, Yankee Minus one-fifteen, Zulu twenty-five. All systems nominal at this time, over.*'

It seemed as if I was falling straight into the planet's violent atmosphere. Forcing my gaze away from the maelstrom, I looked to my right and upward. There, only a few hundred thousand kilometres away, was the pizza-hued orb of Io, the innermost of the Galilean moons, volcanoes spitting hot sulphuric gases above its crimson surface . . .

'*We copy, eight-one-six Victor X-Ray Hotel.*' Geoff Smith-Makepeace's voice was clear and distinct, as if he were sitting just behind me. '*On-board telemetry is good and we've got you on the scope. You're clear for initiation of primary descent sequence, over.*'

Vertical bars bordered my focal plane, their millimetre-marks shifting with each movement of my head, as luminescent digits constantly changed just above my centre of vision. I concentrated on them, trying to make my vertigo go away . . .

'*Thank you*, Medici.' Old Bill again. '*Course corrections entered into primary interface and we're ready for descent burn on the five mark. Five . . . four . . . three . . . two . . . one . . . zero and mark.*'

All at once, the universe itself seemed to roll over on its side. Jupiter and Io swerved away, and for a brief instant I caught a glimpse of the *Medici Explorer*, a tiny elongated spot of light moving against the thin band of Jupiter's ring plane. Then the ship was swept away and I found myself looking at Jupiter again; the planet now was upside-down, the broad off-white patch of its southern pole below me instead of above.

The only thing missing was my stomach: I had left it somewhere behind. Bile rushed up my throat; I choked it down as I reached up and grabbed the smooth plastic sides of the VR helmet between my hands. I managed to yank the helmet off my head before I could vomit. Shutting my eyes, feeling cool air against my sweat-drenched face, I fell out of telepresence and into the chair in which I had been sitting all along.

'You OK?' Young Bill said from behind me. I carefully nodded my head, still keeping my eyes closed. 'OK. All right. Just take it easy. I've got a bag here if you need it.'

I swallowed and relaxed in the chair, breathing deeply until the nausea gradually faded and I felt it was safe to open my eyes again. I was back in the bridge of the *Medici Explorer*, sitting at the engineering station where Montrose and Young Bill had wired me into the VR uplink from the *Marius*. Although Geoff was hunched over his console and the skipper was paying attention only to his board, Betsy had turned around to look at me with worried eyes. Young Bill was standing next to my chair, his arms folded across his chest, and I couldn't help but notice the paper vomit bag held almost out of sight in his left hand. Betsy returned her gaze to her screens, murmuring under her breath as she continued to relay information to the others. Saul's eyes flickered once in my direction, but he said nothing. No one had time to coddle a cybersick passenger.

'Sorry about that.' I swallowed again and wiped cold sweat off my face with my shirt sleeve. 'I was doing fine, then . . . boom, everything flip-flopped on me.'

Young Bill smiled. 'Dad rolled the boat over, that's what got you.

Don't worry about it. Happens to everyone.' He hesitated. 'If you don't want to go back out there . . .'

I shook my head. 'I can handle it. Just need a few minutes to get my act together again.'

Bill didn't reply. He looked away from me, toward the holo-screens arrayed around the bridge. Displayed on a couple of the holos was the same view I had witnessed only a minute ago: the inner Jovian system, as seen through the fibre-optic eyes of Tiger, the AI that was now lashed to the outer hull of the *Marius*.

When I was a kid growing up in a small town in rural Tennessee, there was a German shepherd named Luke who used to ride on top of his master's pickup-truck. Not inside the truck's cab, or even in the bed, but standing on the vehicle's roof like a giant hood-ornament that had been misplaced. If you were driving along the highway, sometimes you caught sight of Luke as his owner's truck went past in the opposite lane, his head cocked forth, his ears spread back by the wind, all four paws planted firmly on the cab roof. No one, least of all his owner, knew why Luke liked to do this, or how he managed to pull off this unique stunt, and I often wondered what the dog saw as he rode through the wind and speed.

'Tiger,' Montrose said softly, 'let's see the ship, please.' The robot instantly obeyed, its upper turret rotating a hundred and eighty degrees and angling downward until, many years later, I had an inkling what it must have been like to see the world through Luke's eyes.

We now saw the boat from the robot's perspective as the *Marius* plunged toward Amalthea. 816-VXH was a long, wasp-waisted spacecraft, a workhorse built for function rather than aesthetics. Most of it was comprised of three liquid-fuel rockets; since the craft was too small for it to carry nuclear engines without burdening it with extra shielding, its designers had compensated by devoting more than half its structure to an immense LuneCorp oxygen-hydrogen engine and two outrigger boosters. In essence, the *Marius* was a collection of engines with a payload section added almost as an afterthought.

As Tiger's cameras rotated from the pale-blue umbra of the engine exhaust, we could see the long, narrow neck of its midsection, leading straight forward until it ended in the wedge-shaped command module at the bow. Empty bolt holes and small pit-marks along the fuselage showed where Tiger had dismantled cargo trusses, a pair of forward-mounted long-range sensor canards and other unnecessary or redundant equipment before the *Marius* had launched from the *Medici Explorer*; even its navigational beacons had been removed to lessen the boat's mass by a few more kilos.

'*Eight one-six Victor X-Ray Hotel, this is one-twelve Whisky Bravo Nebraska,*' Captain Montrose's voice was a dull drone above the electronics chitters and beeps of the bridge. 'Tiger just gave you guys the once over and you're looking good. Don't worry about your hull temp, I don't see any paint bubbling. Over.'

I picked up a headset and listened to Old Bill through the earpiece: '. . . *Roger that,* Medici, *and concur with your opinion. Over.*' One of the screens showed the boat's present position below Jupiter's plasma torus. So far, so good; the *Marius* hadn't been affected by the intense ionization of the belt.

Young Bill's attention was fixed upon the screens. Out there was his first-father, risking his life to save those of two people whom he had never met, and here was his son, left behind to nursemaid a passenger who had trouble keeping dinner in his stomach. The kid was trying to remain cool, but his fists were clenched at his sides, his jaw so tight that his facial muscles twitched. A man-child scared for his father's life, and helpless to do anything about it except watch from the distance.

I felt the memory of the alligator clip's pinch in the palm of my right hand. All I had to worry about was whether I would throw up. I picked up the VR helmet, juggled it reluctantly between my hands, then slid my head once more into its foam-padded maw.

'OK,' I said. 'Ready when you are.'

He gave me a distant glance. 'Whoever said I was ready?'

We came in fast on Amalthea, the boat's engines throttled up to 90 per cent as it struggled against Jupiter's gravity well, Old Bill nursing the manoeuvring thrusters as he sought to remain locked on final approach to the tiny moon. In contrast to Jupiter, Amalthea barely exerted enough gravity to make a landing possible; Smith-Tate had to orbit the potato-shaped rock twice before he was able to bring the *Marius* down close enough to Pan crater for him to achieve touchdown.

The *Marius* skirted the western rim of the crater – through Tiger's eyes I caught the briefest glimpse of the unmanned relay station in the crater's centre as the boat swept over it – and crossed the ninety kilometres to the eastern rim in barely a minute before Old Bill throttled down the engines. I caught a brief glimpse of the *Barnard* – human-made wreckage lying against the crater wall – then the *Marius* swerved around in a half-circle and the landing thrusters kicked up a cloud of red sulphuric dust which obscured Tiger's camera lenses.

It was nearly impossible for me to tell whether we had landed. My only input was Bill's taut voice: '*Twenty metres . . . fifteen metres . . . got some dust in the window, radar still operational . . . ten metres . . . whoa, watch that boulder . . . eight metres . . . thrusters down 10 per cent . . . five metres, two . . .*'

The picture inside my helmet jostled a little, static lines creasing the screen . . . '*OK, touchdown. Engine arm off, grapples deployed and holding, computer reset. One-twelve, this is Marius eight-sixteen, we're down and looking good. Over.*'

Through my helmet, I heard the faint sound of cheering in the bridge. '*Roger that, Victor X-Ray Hotel eight-sixteen.*' Captain Montrose said through the comlink. '*Thanks, Bill, we were about to have heart attacks up here. Over.*'

Yoshio Smith-Tanaka's voice: '*Sorry, Saul, but the doctor's on house-call right now. Take two aspirins and call me in the morning. Over.*'

Relieved laughter over the comlink. Old Bill started going through the post-landing checklist. The dust gradually settled and I was able to take my first good look at Amalthea. The floor of Pan crater stretched away before me, its western rim lost beyond the short horizon and even the relay station a barely distinguishable huddle of domes and antennae in the far distance. All around us were tiny impact craters and pulverized boulders, tinged a dull scarlet by ejecta from Io's volcanoes; the surface vaguely resembled the Martian landscape at twilight.

Amalthea was a cold, ugly little world, precipitously hovering at the edge of its own personal doomsday in Jupiter's gravity well, yet the scenery wasn't what immediately caught my attention. Beyond the horizon, Jupiter itself was an immense black wall across the sky, more vast than anything human eyes had ever seen before. Across its benighted hemisphere, I could see dozens of lightning flashes erupting as giant storms silently thundered within its dense atmosphere, tiny spots which look insignificant until one realizes that each unleashes enough energy to level entire cities on Earth.

Most frightening of all, the planet looked as if it were falling toward us. Even though I cognitively knew that this was an optical illusion caused by Amalthea's slow rotation and that I was in no immediate danger, I had the impulse to flee, to run like hell from that staggering black mass in the sky . . . and yet, like a deer on a country highway that has been transfixed by the headlights of an approaching vehicle, I could not turn my eyes away.

Such was my fascination that I didn't realize that I was being spoken to through the comlink until Old Bill whistled sharply. '*Hey, Cole!*' he snapped. '*Stop sight-seeing! We got a job to do down here!*'

I shut my eyes, making a conscious effort to break the spell. 'I'm here,' I said. 'Sorry. What do you want me to do?'

'*Nothing except stop playing with my robot.*' He paused, then I heard him murmur as if he was speaking to Yoshio, '*Drat, I knew it was a bad idea to let him run Tiger . . .*'

Saul's voice broke into the comlink '*Elliot, we need to disengage you from active control of Tiger. You'll still be able to monitor, but Bill's going to take control while he inspects the* Barnard.'

Smith-Tate's voice again: '*Hey, skipper, whatever we're going to do, we better do it quick. My computer says we're going to lose telemetry in fifteen minutes when you guys begin the slingshot. Over.*'

A short pause, then Montrose's voice returned. '*Damn, you're right. I thought we had more time than that. What happened to our window? Over.*'

Old Bill: '*Dad-gum landing was trickier than we thought, that's what happened. Lost time on those flybys. Like I said, we got about fifteen minutes until you begin your periapsis manoeuvre and we lose your signal. I could handle Tiger from down here, but it would just tie me up and I'd lose EVA time. Rather you did it from up there. You copy? Over.*'

Another pause, then Montrose's voice returned: '*We copy,* Marius, *and we're on the case. Geoff's going to run Tiger from up here. Elliot, you're out of the loop as of now. Over.*'

'Right,' I said, 'I understand.' By then a red bar had appeared across the top of my screen: 'MANUAL DISENGAGE/19:24:36/ 103692'. A few seconds later the robot's head revolved of its own accord and I found myself looking at the wreckage of the *Barnard*.

The *Marius* had touched down barely thirty metres from the *Barnard* – a considerable feat of flying on Old Bill's part, considering the difficulties he had encountered just getting to Amalthea in the first place. The *Barnard* was a near-duplicate of the *Marius*, and it was remarkable that any of the shuttle's crew had survived the crash: the craft looked like a toy spaceship that had been trampled during a sandbox tantrum by an angry brat. Although the command module had remained intact, the shuttle's spine was broken, its outrigger rockets sheared away and its landing skids twisted almost beyond recognition. Worst of all, the main airlock hatch was buried beneath the debris; it was apparent that the emergency escape hatch atop of the command module would have to be used.

'*OK, one-twelve, I'm suiting up now,*' Old Bill said. '*Yoshio's decompressing the airlock and standing by to assist the survivors. Send Tiger in. Over.*'

'*We copy, eight-sixteen, over.*' This time it was Geoff Smith-Makepeace's voice over the comlink. There was another brief pause, then Tiger began to move, its claw manipulators unsnapping the cables which had secured it to the boat's fuselage. Once that was done, Tiger walked down the length of the *Marius* until it reached the starboard-bow landing gear; I grabbed the armrests of my seats, instinctively holding on against its lurching gait.

It took a couple of minutes for Geoff to guide Tiger down the leg of the landing gear; the robot had been principally designed for zero-gee activity, so even Amalthea's weak gravity gave it some problems. Once it reached the ground, though, it scuttled quickly across the rocky surface until it reached the *Barnard*.

It didn't take Tiger long to clamber on to the shuttle's upper fuselage, but once it reached the escape hatch another problem was encountered: its handle was broken, making it impossible for Tiger to open the hatch from the outside. Montrose talked to Casey Nimersheim and instructed her how to fire the pyros which would blow the emergency hatch, yet when the scientist repeatedly toggled the switch, nothing happened. Bill and Geoff decided to have Tiger cut through the hatch. Tiger's blunt laser-arm swung into position above the hatch, then tiny globules of melted alloy spurted away as the invisible beam lanced into the groove between the hatch-cover and the fuselage.

At the periphery of my vision, I could see the dull gleam of emergency lamps through the shattered windows of the cockpit. The windows were much too narrow for anyone to crawl through, but I caught a glimpse of a spacesuited figure looking out for a moment, taking a quick peek at Tiger – and, by extension, me – until it retreated into the command module's shielded interior from the lethal radiation outside the shuttle.

'*OK, one-twelve, I'm through my airlock. Over.*' At the sound of Old Bill's voice, Tiger's head turned around until I was looking back toward the *Marius*. I saw a large, fat silhouette against the searchlight's bright corona: Smith-Tate's radiation-proof exo-skeleton, advancing toward the *Barnard*.

'*We copy, eight-sixteen.*' This time it was Betsy's soft voice over the comlink. '*Please be advised that neither of the survivors are wearing hardsuits. Repeat, neither of them are in hardsuits, only flight gear. Once you get them out, you're going to have to make it quick . . .*'

Montrose abruptly cut in: '*Bill, we've got three minutes until communications blackout. After that, you and Yoshio are on your own. Do you copy? Over.*'

'*Shit, Oh, shit . . .*' It was the first time I heard Old Bill use profanity; the tension of the operation had overwhelmed his Mormon asceticism. No wonder; he was now faced with two more immediate problems.

First, since neither Nimersheim nor the critically injured Bellafonte were wearing radiation armour, they would both be subjected to Jupiter's radiation the moment they left the shuttle. Unless a quick transfer was made to the *Marius*, their rescue would be futile: the REMs they would receive if they lingered for very long on Amalthea's surface would kill them just as surely as if they had died in the crash.

Second, the radio link between the *Medici Explorer* and the *Marius* was about to be lost. Although Yoshio could conceivably take control of Tiger, the time wasted while he jacked into telepresence would slow down the rescue operation considerably . . . and, with each minute that passed, the window for the orbital rendezvous between the *Marius* and the *Medici Explorer* was narrowed even further.

'*Geoff, how's Tiger doing up here?*' It was getting harder to hear Old Bill; the comlink was becoming rough with static. '*Are you through that hatch yet? Over.*'

Tiger's head rotated back to the upper fuselage of the *Barnard*. The view was becoming increasingly scratchy, yet I could see that the laser had almost completely made its way around the circumference of the hatch. '*We're almost through,*' Geoff said, '*but I don't see any signs of it giving. Should be sagging by now, but it isn't. Something's still holding it in place. Maybe the gaskets we melted froze up again, I dunno . . .*'

'*Bill, this is Saul.*' The skipper suddenly sounded tired. '*If the hatch doesn't give . . . I don't know.*' A long pause. '*You might have to give it up. You gotta get yourselves out of there . . .*'

'*No sir, we're not.*' Smith-Tate's voice was determined. '*We didn't come all this way just to give up now.*'

I couldn't see him, but I guessed Old Bill was standing beside the *Barnard*, just below Tiger. If so, he couldn't climb up to the hatch because the robot was in the way. Chaos theory in action: problems breeding more problems, everything sliding down a slippery slope.

Saul: '*Bill . . .*'

Bill: '*Shut up, skipper . . . Geoff, listen to me. As soon as you cut through the hatch, get Tiger to jump on it!*'

Geoff: '*What . . .? Eight-sixteen, we don't copy, please repeat . . .*'

Betsy: '*One minute until blackout.*'

Bill: '*You heard me. Make Tiger jump on the hatch. Maybe it'll kick the damn . . . durn thing in.*'

The laser was only a couple of centimetres short of finishing its work and I couldn't detect any sign of the hatch buckling. Telemetry between Amalthea and the *Medici Explorer* was becoming increasingly furry: it was hard to make out Bill's voice through my headphones, and thin bands were beginning to race across my field of vision.

Geoff: '*Umm . . . we copy, eight-sixteen, but that would probably trash Tiger . . .*'

Bill: '*Screw the 'bot, just do it*'

Saul: '*Do what he says. We're running out of time . . .*'

The torch reached the end of its path; there was now a blackened circle running through the edge of the emergency hatch, yet it stubbornly remained shut.

Bill: '*Do it, boy! Jump!*'

A second later Tiger lurched forward into the ragged circle the laser had traced, placing its full weight upon the hatch.

In the next instant I felt the surface of my world collapse beneath me, saw a flurry of motion, then the scene within the VR helmet blacked out to be briefly replaced by random test-patterns and numeric codes before everything went stark grey, and all I heard was Old Bill's voice shouting through screeching static: *'It's through! It's . . .'*

Then the comlink went dead.

'Eight-one-six Victor X-Ray Hotel, this is one-twelve Whisky Bravo Nebraska, do you copy, over . . . Eight-one-six Victor X-Ray Hotel, this is one-twelve Whisky Bravo Nebraska. Do you copy? Over.'

An hour and fifty-six minutes after telemetry with the *Marius* was lost, the *Medici Explorer* had successfully completed its flyby of Jupiter. The vessel had slingshot around the planet's farside, following an elliptical trajectory which had begun near Jupiter's south pole and ended above its north pole, bringing the ship within 100,000 kilometres of its stratosphere before it shot around the planet's vast limb. The polar flyby had kept the *Explorer* out of the plasma torus between Jupiter and Io; even though we were now only 300,000 klicks from the planet, there had been very little buffeting when the ship entered the magnetotail extending away from Jupiter's leeside.

Yet we had not heard from the *Marius* since the beginning of the blackout almost two hours ago. Although this could be attributed to electromagnetic interference, the fact of the matter was that the crew had no way of knowing what had happened down on Amalthea. Although we were close above the tiny moon's orbit, Amalthea itself was now on the other side of the planet and thus out of reach of our transmissions. The *Marius* would have lifted off from the moon by now, according to the rescue plan, and should be climbing the gravity well for its rendezvous with the *Medici Explorer*.

That's what should have been happening. Here we were, though, in the right place at the right time, and there was no *Marius* to be seen or heard. There was only one correct way for William Smith-Tate to bring the boat back home . . . and a thousand different ways for him to go wrong.

'Eight-sixteen Victor X-Ray Hotel, this is Medici Explorer, one-twelve Whisky Bravo Nebraska. Please come in, over . . .'

Geoff's voice was raw. He had not left the bridge since he had been woken out of bed by Young Bill almost twenty hours ago, and as we neared the end of the third shift it was apparent that he had reached the verge of total collapse. His first-wife Betsy was not doing much better; she had been awake longer than Geoff and there were now dark circles under her eyes. Yet both of them had refused to leave the bridge, even when Saul had given them direct orders to go below and get some rest; at best, they had catnapped in the rest alcove for a few minutes before dragging themselves back to their duty stations. Now Betsy wearily slumped over her console, watching the radar screens, while Geoff repeatedly recited the same call-signs over and over, his voice becoming a little more hoarse with each repetition.

If this was mutiny, then it wasn't the sort of insubordination a captain could fight, and Saul Montrose wasn't inclined to hold captain's mast. He had not sat in his chair since the completion of the periapsis burn nearly an hour ago; instead, he had paced the bridge and slugged down reheated coffee until he loudly proclaimed he was giving up on the stuff because he was just pissing it away. No one laughed; everyone had reached, and passed, the point of exhaustion. Now there were only unspoken fears and sick-at-stomach feelings of helplessness.

Leslie Smith-Tanaka had escorted Wendy and Kaneko to bed before returning to the bridge with a bag of doughnuts from the galley. The doughnuts had gone uneaten and Wendy did not stay put; she meekly returned to the bridge in her pyjamas, saying that she could not sleep, and none of the adults were in the mood to argue. Wendy took a chair in the rest alcove next to her Aunt Lynn, who had been on the bridge since the beginning of the mission, watching the holoscreens and rarely saying anything to anyone. When Wendy fell asleep against her shoulder, Lynn Smith-Tate had cradled the child's head in her lap and covered her with her sweater, but her eyes had seldom left the screens.

That left only Young Bill. He had been inside one of the observation blisters during the flyby and burn manoeuvre, and I had expected him to man the telescope until his father returned. When Geoff failed to re-establish contact with the *Marius* when anticipated, Bill had climbed out of the blister and, without saying a word to anyone, left the bridge. By the time the ship's chronometer flashed 2200, Saul walked over to me and asked if I would mind going below to find him.

'He needs someone to talk to,' he whispered, 'and neither his mom nor I are up to that right now.' He handed me a headset, which I clamped around my neck. 'I'll let you know when anything changes up here.'

Finding Young Bill was easier than I expected; although my first thought was to try the Smith-Tate quarters in Arm One, I anticipated searching the entire vessel for him. Yet no sooner had I left the bridge and was climbing down the hub access ladder toward the carousel when I heard a soft, rythmic pounding sound from the other side of a hatch just below the bridge. I thought it was a normal mechanical noise until it made a peculiar double-beat and I recognized it for what it was: the bouncing of a rubber ball.

The hatch was marked 'STORES 1'; beyond it was a small compartment whose walls were lined with recessed metal drawers and cabinets, each marked with the names of various items: food rations, clothing, medical supplies, tools and spare parts and so forth. The bouncing ceased as soon as I undogged the hatch and swung it open; Bill lay against the far wall where he had used an elastic strap and two grommets to secure himself, and he was holding a frayed yellow tennis ball in his hands.

We stared at each other for a few moments, each mildly surprised to see the other, neither of us knowing quite what to say. I then noticed a small handwritten sign taped to the ceiling just above his head: 'No Handball in this Area!'

'Pardon me, is this the handball court?' I asked as straight-faced as I could. 'I thought it was the swimming pool.'

The corners of Young Bill's mouth ticked upward for a moment; he followed my gaze to the sign and shook his head. 'Dad hates it when I do this . . . says it leaves marks on the walls.' His smile disappeared. 'Want to close the door? I'm kinda busy at the moment.'

I shut the hatch, but not before I pulled myelf into the storeroom and grabbed a ceiling rail. An annoyed expression crossed his face, but he didn't protest. I looked at the ball in his hands. 'I tried handball once,' I said. 'When I lived in Washington and belonged to the downtown Y . . .'

He blinked. 'The Y?'

68

'The YMCA,' I added, but he still looked confused; nothing like that on the Moon. 'Young Men's Christian Association. Sort of a club. They've got great gyms.'

'Oh . . . yeah. I've heard of them.' His fingers absently traced the stitching of the tennis ball. 'Never been to one, sorry.'

He continued to stare pensively at the ball. I cleared my throat. 'Not exactly a regulation court, but I guess it's good enough for practice.'

He responded by suddenly hurling the ball at the hatch, missing me by less than a metre. It ricocheted between the floor and the hatch, shot up and hit the ceiling, then sailed straight back into his left hand. 'Nice shot,' I said.

Young Bill cupped the ball within his hands and was quiet for a couple of minutes, gazing at the ball as if it was all that mattered. 'You know,' he said after a while, 'I don't think people back there . . . back on Earth, I mean . . . I don't think they know what it's really like out here.'

'They know it's dangerous,' I said. 'I knew that even before I decided to do this story.'

He shook his head. 'No . . . no, they really don't know. They think they know it's dangerous, but they really can't have a real idea what it's like to . . .'

He paused, letting out his breath as he idly tossed the ball back and forth between his hands. 'You asked Aunt Betsy last night about what it's like for Wendy not to have a normal childhood, but you didn't ask me.'

I shook my head but didn't say anything. 'I think a normal childhood,' Bill went on, 'is when your father goes off to work and you know for certain that he's coming back alive at the end of the day . . . but I wouldn't know, because it's never been that way for me.'

'Do you wish you had a normal childhood?' I asked.

Bill shrugged. 'Too late for that now.' He paused again. 'Yeah, man. I wish I had a normal, happy, stupid childhood, no matter what Aunt Betsy says about the joys of being a precocious kid. In fact, I want it so bad, I don't think I'm going to stay around here anymore.'

'Your mom told me this afternoon you were thinking about jumping ship and going to college on Earth.'

'Yep.' A smile briefly crossed his face. 'In fact, I'm more than just thinking about it. Before we left the Moon, I got a fax from the University of Edinburgh. They've accepted me for early admission into the undergrad programme. The last thing I did before we split Descartes City was transfer the first year's tuition from my savings. So it's done . . . I'm in. One month after we get back, I'm off to Scotland.'

He gave me a sharp look. The folks don't know about it yet,' he said. 'I'm going to tell them after this run is over, but do me a favour and don't let on, OK?'

'Don't worry,' I said. 'I won't tell them, I promise.' Bill nodded his head and bounced the tennis ball off the wall again. 'Congratulations,' I added. 'I'm glad you got in. What are you going to study?'

'I dunno.' Again the fleeting smile. 'I told them I wanted into the astronomy school so they'd give my application a second look, but it's going to be anything but, y'know. I'm sick of astronomy. Sick of space.' He shrugged again. 'I just want to live in Scotland for a while, that's all.

'I've been there,' I said. 'You'll like Edinburgh. It's got a giant castle overlooking the city. Every day at noon they fire the cannon from the inner keep for the tourists. You can see the Firth of Forth from up there.'

'Sounds pretty mondo.' He hesitated. 'Dad's going to be pretty pissed when he hears the news. He wants me to step into his shoes, be a space engineer and so forth, but I dunno . . . I've talked college with him before and he wants me to go to Brigham Young, but I can't get jazzed about living in Salt Lake City.'

'Not the same thing.'

'Uh-uh.' He laughed drily. 'I mean, I've been to Utah, or at least as far as Salt Lake. When you stop and think about it, it's not much different than living on the Moon. I couldn't take that for . . .'

He stopped short, listening to an invisible voice, as I simultaneously heard the forgotten headset around my neck begin to whisper to me. I yanked the headset to my ears in time to hear Geoff's voice.

'. . . *X-Ray Hotel, this is* Medici Explorer, *we're standing by. Please repeat, over.*'

There was a short pause, then William Smith-Tate's voice came over the comlink: '*Roger that, one-twelve Whisky Bravo Nebraska, this is* Marius *eight-sixteen. We've got you on the scope and we're coming in, bearing X-Ray minus six-two, Yankee eleven, Zulu minus five-point-five-two. Over.*'

As Young Bill cupped his hands over his ears, listening to his father's distant voice through the subcutaneous comlink, there were hints of mixed emotions in his face. Relief, yes – his father was alive and coming home – and astonishment.

Yet, even though he would have been the last to admit it, there was also the slightest twinge of regret.

'*Marius, this is one-twelve Whisky Bravo . . . aw, hell, Bill, we're glad to see you. Can you give us your present condition, please? Over.*'

'*Affirmative, one-twelve. We've got one . . . repeat, one . . . survivor. Sorry, but we lost a man down there.*' A short pause. '*Yoshio and I are OK. So's Dr Nimersheim. Sorry for the delay, it was a rough flight. Eight-sixteen* Marius *over.*'

'The co-pilot didn't make it.' I said.

'Uh-huh.' Young Bill was already unfastening the straps; he opened a drawer and stashed the tennis ball under a stack of folded jumpsuits, like a kid on Earth hiding a pack of joints from his father. 'I better get down to the airlock to help him and Uncle Yoshi out of the boat.'

'You don't sound all that surprised,' I said.

Young Bill shut the drawer. 'Like I said . . . my father always comes home after work.' In the instant that he looked my way before he vaulted across the compartment toward the hatch, there was silent desperation – and defiance – in his eyes.

'Always has,' he finished. 'Always will.'

The Catacombs of Valhalla

ONCE THE *Marius* had rendezvoused and docked with the *Medici Explorer*, Old Bill and Yoshio Smith-Tanaka took Casey Nimersheim straight to the infirmary on Deck 1-A. The shuttle's co-pilot, Marlon Bellafonte, had died shortly after liftoff from Amalthea; the doctor had pronounced him dead from injuries sustained during the shuttle crash plus the stress of being hastily moved from the *Barnard* to the *Marius*. At least the rescue party had been able to bring Bellafonte's body back to the *Explorer*; they had been unable to prise Wayne Reese's corpse from the wreckage before the launch-window shut, and Old Bill was forced to leave the shuttle pilot on Amalthea.

Nimersheim, though, was in reasonably good health and spirits, considering the ordeal she had suffered. Once Yoshio had examined her and tended the few minor cuts and bruises she had suffered, he administered a sedative which put her to sleep for the next eight hours. However, when the doctor checked her suit dosimeter, he discovered that the amount of radiation to which the young woman had been exposed while marooned on Amalthea had reached seventy-two REMs. The maximum number of REMs allowed per annum under union health regulations is seventy-five. Although she was still safe from contracting leukaemia, she couldn't expect to continue working in the Jovian system; a single EVA, even in the outer fringes of the system, would certainly push her over the limit.

This discovery prompted Yoshio to check both Old Bill's and his own dosimeters. More bad news. Since Yoshio himself had never left the *Marius*, he had received barely five REMs during the mission, well within the safety limits – but Old Bill, even though he had been protected by his exoskeleton, had received almost twenty REMs. Under the same union codes, the maximum radiation exposure allowed within a thirty-day period is twenty-five REMs, with a career limit of four hundred REMs.

In the parlance of pro spacers, William Smith-Tate had been singed. If he had been cooked, his career would have been automatically over and he would have to spend the rest of his life grounded on Earth; if he had been fried, he would have already been dying in the infirmary. Considering the circumstances, he was lucky to have been only singed – yet for the next month he could not leave the vessel under any circumstances save for the most dire emergency.

At risk was not only his own health, but also his EVA certification. The rules are necessarily tough, because otherwise the major insurance companies – chief among them Lloyd's of London, ConSpace's principal guarantor – would refuse to underwrite industrial space efforts. Indeed, after a spacer receives more than four hundred REMs, Pax Astra automatically rescinds that person's EVA certification . . . and a spacer who can't step outside of an airlock might as well ship back to Earth, his or her career over and with little more than a pension on the horizon.

By the time Yoshio broke the bad news to Old Bill, though, most of the crew had gone to sleep. Exhausted both physically and emotionally, they had been able to do little more than greet Old Bill and Yoshio at the airlock before they succumbed to fatigue. Leslie and Lynn hauled Bellafonte's body, still encased in his spacesuit, out of the *Marius* and took it to the same storage compartment where I had found Young Bill playing handball, where they lashed the corpse to a bulkhead for the time being. Saul Montrose and Young Bill returned to the bridge where they assumed fourth watch by double-checking the systems to make certain the ship was secure and en route to Callisto and putting everything in the control of the computers. After they relieved Betsy and Geoff from duty, the two men retired to the rest alcove where they buckled themselves into armchairs and sacked out for the next six hours.

By then, I was back in my seldom-visited quarters down on Deck 1-E, snuggled into my bunk and feeling the comfortable pull of gravity for the first time in many hours. The shields had been raised from my compartment window. As I had the ship-morning before, I spent my last waking moments gazing out of the portal. This time, though, I couldn't see Jupiter at all; although the vessel was still close to the giant planet, it was now receding behind us as the *Medici Explorer* headed out-system toward Callisto, and all I could see was faint starlight and the tiny orbs of the Galilean moons.

I fell asleep believing that the hardest part of the voyage was over, never once thinking that the worst was yet to come.

By 18.00 hours ship-time the following day, the *Medici Explorer* was on final approach to Callisto, where it was scheduled to be reunited with its convoy. If the crew had thought their troubles to be over, however, they were in for a rude – although not entirely unanticipated – surprise: the drone freighters were being held hostage by Valhalla Station.

More precisely, the consignment of helium-3 which was supposed to be loaded aboard the three vessels had been embargoed. The liquidated gas was still being held within the underground storage tanks at Valhalla, even though the convoy had arrived at Callisto more than twenty-four hours earlier while the rescue operation was still underway; the station's dock crews had yet to pump it into the barges that would ferry the precious payload from the moon's surface up to orbit.

Given the fact that the *Medici Explorer* was already running two days behind schedule, the situation threatened to further narrow the window for the convoy's return to Earth. Yet when Saul Montrose – fully rested by now, having slept, showered and dressed in fresh clothes – inquired by comlink why the load-up had been delayed, he was told by Valhalla's duty officer that the matter would be discussed when the station's general manager, B.F. LeRoy, arrived aboard the *Medici Explorer*. He was coming up on a shuttle with the local pilot – an astrogator who customarily helped guide deep-space vessels into parking orbit – and the issue would be discussed then. The duty officer then signed off without so much as a word of apology.

When I caught up with Saul, he was in the wardroom on Deck 1-F, finishing a late dinner. Swamp, the AI that resided in the mess deck, was happily scurrying away into the adjacent galley with the tray that Montrose had placed on the floor for it to retrieve, and Saul was relaxing with a mug of coffee before returning to the bridge. Through the wardroom window we could see the cratered and ice-covered surface of Callisto, the vast equatorial bull's-eye of Valhalla Basin prominent at the moon's equator.

'The company warned me there might be problems with station management on this trip,' Montrose said. He was more amused than irritated. 'Last time out, the captain was presented with a larger invoice than was stipulated in the contract. The freighters had already been loaded by then, of course, so there wasn't much Butt Face . . .'

'Who?'

Montrose smiled. 'LeRoy's nickname, from back when he ran Arsia Station on Mars. B.F. stands for Brock Francis, but we used to call him Butt Face when I did the Mars run.' He shrugged. 'He used to pull the same thing back then, trying to hold back delivery of goods until he and his crew got the perks they wanted. Didn't always get him very far, but at least he's consistent.'

I shook my head. 'I don't understand. Since he's also employed by ConSpace . . .'

'He works for the company, yeah, but remember where he and his people are coming from. These are folks many millions of kilometres from the front office. Out here, guys tend to figure they can make their own rules and nobody's going to say boo to them.' Montrose sipped his coffee. 'Same spirit that got the Pax started in the first place. They're just after a bigger slice of the pie, that's all.'

'And the fact that you just rescued one of their crew doesn't matter to them?'

'Not really, no. Not when it comes to this.' The captain gazed out of the window as Callisto swept past us once again. 'I suppose they're grateful, sure, but LeRoy probably had this little scheme cooked up months ago. If I know him, he's not going to let a little gratitude get in his way.'

'So what are you going to do about it?'

Montrose sighed and placed the empty mug on the floor. As Swamp scampered in to get it – '*Dirty cup! Swamp found a dirty cup to wash! Thank you, thank you!*' – he stood up from the table, stretched, and hitched up his belt.

'The way I figure it,' he said, 'these guys want to play poker. OK, then . . . let's see who has the best hand.'

A half hour later, the shuttle *Morabito* from Valhalla Station rendezvoused with the *Medici Explorer* and docked in its auxiliary berth. After its two passengers cycled through the airlock, Young Bill escorted them to the bridge where Saul and Betsy were patiently waiting for them. The local pilot, a pale young woman named Jamie Van Sant, was no stranger to either the *Explorer* or its crew; she and Betsy retreated to the rest alcove to share coffee and conversation, leaving Saul to deal with B.F. LeRoy.

To say that there was a confrontation between Montrose and LeRoy would be to imply hostility between the two men. LeRoy stood two metres in height; in Earth-normal gravity, he would have weighed in at almost 140 kilos. He had a sloppy, ill-trimmed moustache and a stubbled face looked as if he dry-razored his beard once every few days; there were large sweat-stains beneath the armpits of his shirt and vest, and his breath held the sweet-sour odour of liquor hastily chastened by mints. Everything about him suggested a lifelong bully, just civilized enough to get a decent job.

Yet never once did the GMs voice raise; he was savvy enough to know that posturing or making threats would get him nowhere. As Saul had told me in the mess deck, they had encountered each other before; the two men plainly didn't like each other, but they could negotiate, at least for the time being. They shook hands with easy familiarity, made some smalltalk, then got down to brass tacks.

To summarize: LeRoy, speaking on behalf of his crew, did not believe that Valhalla Station was receiving adequate compensation for its hard work, and therefore the base personnel was collectively demanding a raise in the net percentage of gross profits received by ConSpace from the sale of helium-3 on Earth.

Saul demurred to the argument, yet held firm against the demands; yes, he agreed that Valhalla Station probably deserved a bigger piece of the action, but his opinion didn't really matter because this was an issue that had to be settled between Callisto and ConSpace's board of directors. As a lowly deep-space captain, responsible for little more than shepherding a bunch of freighters from the Moon to Jupiter and back again, it was not his place to rewrite company policy.

Perhaps not, replied LeRoy, but since ConSpace's board of directors had ignored his petitions thus far, the time had come for him to demonstrate his disgust in a more direct fashion. Unless Montrose himself forged an agreement-in-principal for a larger share of the profits to be given to Valhalla's personnel, the current consignment of helium-3 would not be loaded aboard the freighters, and the convoy could return to Earth with empty holds for all he cared.

'Nothing personal, Saul,' he said, 'but, after all, business is business.'

Montrose played with his elegant moustache while he pretended to weigh the alternatives. Of course, he said after a few moments, if you don't give us the helium-3, we're under no obligation to reciprocate by unloading your own supplies. Saul then picked up a datapad and recited the outbound cargo manifest: fresh produce, medical supplies, spare engine parts and various personal-request items including a new billiards-table cover and several boxes of current recreational VR chips, along with various packages from families and friends back home, including one crate which was listed as 'CTB Bibles' – 'Claimed To Be Bibles,' and therefore unopened although the crate had rattled in a way which was more akin to bottles than copies of the Holy Scripture.

LeRoy frowned while Montrose read the list, yet he remained stubborn. 'We can do without some of these things,' he said when the captain had finished, 'and if you refuse to surrender the vital necessities, then the *Medici Explorer* will be in direct violation of Pax Astra statutes regarding the withholding of aid to distressed colonists. Laws,' he added smugly, 'which could result in the revocation of a ship's charter and her captain's licence.'

'True enough,' Montrose said. 'Then perhaps we should yield to higher authority.' He then touched his jaw and asked Yoshio Smith-Tanaka to bring one of the *Explorer*'s passengers, Marianne Tillis, to the bridge.

'Who's that?' LeRoy asked.

'The new general manager,' Saul replied. 'Why, you mean the company didn't tell you? Sorry, B.F., but you've been terminated.'

Butt Face's mouth was still agape by the time his replacement arrived on the bridge. Marianne Tillis was a short, stocky woman in her late forties, with a quiet air of determination which stood out in contrast to LeRoy's redneck sleaze. Since she had been revived from biostasis only a few hours earlier, she was still hungover and uncertain of her movements; Yoshio had to guide her to Montrose's empty chair before she was able to relax.

Despite her condition, though, Tillis's mind and tongue were sharp. She presented the stunned LeRoy with a sheaf of documents from ConSpace that officially designated her as the new general manager of Valhalla Station, signed by the company's CEO and directors. She then curtly informed LeRoy that, if he refused to relinquish his command or if the station's personnel refused to carry out their duties, all previously acquired salaries and bonuses would be immediately annulled and no one on Callisto would receive zip for their work.

And that, she said, was the end of the discussion.

LeRoy's jaw worked soundlessly for a few moments before he managed to speak again, and then the first thing he wanted to know was why he hadn't been informed in advance.

He hadn't been told, Tillis replied, because he couldn't be trusted to act in good faith.

LeRoy persisted. What about his job? His career?

Tillis shook her head. His job now belonged to her, she told him, and if he didn't co-operate, his career would end with him operating a regolith combine at Descartes City. He was going home in a zombie tank aboard the *Medici Explorer*, period.

She dismissed him with a wave of her hand. 'You can take the shuttle back to the base to pack your bags and say goodbye to your crew,' she said. 'Sorry, buddy, but you're out of here.'

Still looking as if he had been socked in the skull with a bag of pennies, B.F. LeRoy was led off the bridge by Young Bill, who was trying to hide his grin as he took the pirate down to the mess for a mug of coffee. As soon as he was gone, Tillis reopened the comlink to Valhalla Station. After she introduced herself to the no-longer-smug duty officer, she ordered the immediate loading of helium-3 on to the barges.

After she signed off, Jamie Van Sant – who had been quietly observing the whole scene from the rest alcove – calmly unbuckled her seat belt, pushed herself across the bridge to the navigation console and, after politely introducing herself to Marianne Tillis, began laying in the co-ordinates for the *Medici Explorer*'s parking orbit near its freighters. She performed her duties as local pilot without question or argument.

She knew the score. One boss was as good as another . . . and, after all, business was business.

The fallout of the firing of B.F. LeRoy was that shore leave was shorter than usual. Even though LeRoy's dismissal had been predestined the moment Tillis had boarded the vessel, the thirty men and women who lived and worked at Valhalla Station held Saul Montrose and the crew of the *Medici Explorer* directly accountable. This was discovered when the *Marius* landed on Callisto early the next day.

Six of us rode the ship's boat down from orbit to Valhalla Station: Captain Montrose, Yoshio and Leslie Smith-Tanaka, Lynn Smith-Tate, Young Bill and myself. We left almost half of the ship's company behind. Callisto's one-seventh gravity would have meant that Geoff and Betsy Smith-Makepeace would have had to return to their wheelchairs. Rather than suffer that indignity, they elected, as usual, to stand watch on the *Medici Explorer*. For the first time they were joined, albeit reluctantly, by Old Bill; since Yoshio had restricted him from leaving the vessel for at least another month, he had stayed behind to babysit Wendy and Kaneko.

The *Marius* was not the first shuttle to leave the *Explorer*. When Van Sant had departed from the ship, flying the *Morabito* down to Valhalla Station almost ten hours earlier, she had taken with her three passengers. Marianne Tillis and Karl Hess had already been shuttled down; Hess had been only too happy to leave the vessel aboard which he had made his unwelcome passage to Jupiter, and Tillis was ready to assume her new duties as general manager. Although LeRoy wanted to collect his few personal belongings before shipping out on the *Medici Explorer*, Casey Nimersheim wasn't given that option: she was still recuperating from her ordeal in the infirmary and couldn't risk more REM exposure by leaving the *Explorer*. She had asked her former boss to pack her bags for her.

The base on Callisto is located in the centre of the Valhalla Basin, a vast crater formed millenia ago by the impact of a small asteroid upon the planetoid's ice-encrusted surface. Since Callisto is almost two million kilometres from Jupiter, the moon's orbit lies beyond the most lethal zone of the planet's radiation belts, and the abundance of ice on its frozen surface has assured the small outpost a natural supply of oxygen, water, and liquid-fuel volatiles. In that respect, at least, Valhalla Station is more self-sufficient than even Descartes City, since the lunar colony depends on asteroid farming for its water supply.

Once the *Marius* had touched down on the outskirts of the base, we suited up, decompressed in the airlock, and tramped down the boatramp to the moon's surface. The ground was like dirty snow, brownish-white and crunchy underfoot, eerily similar to a New England pasture during the mid-spring thaw between winter and the beginning of mud season except that the ambient temperature hovered a couple of hundred degrees below zero Celsius. Save for the scores of meteorite craters all around us and the low ridges of the basin in the distance, the floor of the vast basin was nearly flat; Jupiter hung above the horizon as a multicoloured three-quarter sphere the size of a soccer ball held at arm's length, and in the starry black sky I could see Ganymede and Europa as tiny spheroids, Callisto's sisters in the eternal night.

There was a quiet majesty to Callisto which was absent from Amalthea. Here was simple wonder, the awesome beauty one commonly associates with the Jovian system. Yet amid the geodesic domes, nuclear generators, and parabolic antennae, there were mounds of trash that had been carelessly heaped outside airlocks: worn-out hardsuit segments, coils of frayed wiring, torn sheets of insulation, cannibalized robots, plastic this-and-that, unrecognizable garbage. Junk which might have been recycled or landfilled anywhere else, unable to biodegrade in the airless environment.

This was depressing enough, and Young Bill had already hinted at an attitude that was manifest within the base, yet I was unprepared for the dismal squalor of its surface catacombs.

Once we entered one of the domes and cycled through the airlock, we took turns in the tiny ready-room, shedding our hardsuits for the comfort of the fleece-lined jumpsuits Leslie had carried in a duffel bag from the *Marius*. The air inside the EVA chamber was chilly; we could see our breath when we exhaled, and it didn't get much warmer as we climbed down the long ladder into the base's underground warrens.

The stench hit us as soon as Saul opened the hatch to let us into the main tunnel, a dozen odours trapped in the badly filtered air. Sweat and dust, unwashed laundry, overcooked food, raw alcohol, tobacco and marijuana smoke, urine and faeces, something I couldn't identify but which smelled like burnt paper – this and more. Compared to the scrupulously clean confines of the *Medici Explorer*, the tunnel we stepped into reeked like a sewage drain.

The narrow, serpentine corridor was badly lit, its rock walls grimy with handprints and scrawled with obscene graffiti. The conduits running along the low ceiling were battered, their insulation ripped and leaking sickly yellow fibre. Open hatchways revealed quarters with unmade bunks, nude posters, clothes-lines haphazardly suspended between lockers whose doors had been left ajar. Ceiling fixtures flickered inconstantly; discarded cans and food wrappers littered the hard floors. Here, behind the rec-room hatch, four men with oily hair and unkempt beards played five card stud with a small pile of hand-rolled cigarettes as their stakes. There, in a dishevelled laboratory where an empty centrifuge whirled as a creaky ornament, a bald man stared at the image of a complex molecule rotating on a computer screen; the back of his chair was turned toward us, but he seemed to be playing with himself. Loud music – industrial rock, old jazz, wheezy Italian opera – murmured or blasted from each carved-out room we passed, as if each was a different cell in which a seedy reflection of distant Earth was reflected.

Everything within Valhalla Station reflected desperation and loneliness, targetless anger and restrained sorrow, ugly mirth and – most of all – unrelenting boredom. At the edge of the human frontier, the farthest reach of humankind's conquest of the solar system, lay a slum.

We found Marianne Tillis in the general manager's office, located at the end of the main tunnel near the mess hall, where the worst of the boiled-cabbage stench seemed to congregate. Her new office was in shambles: stacks of dusty computer printout lay in collapsing piles across the floor, buried beneath crusty food trays and dog-eared service manuals. Empty litre bottles litered the desk and floor; one half-full bottle on a shelf contained what smelled like pure-grain alcohol. A defunct AI rested against the wall in one corner of the room, its eye-stalks smashed and its pincers ripped away; 'Stupid' had been scrawled in red ink across its carapace.

Tillis was seated at the desk, talking into a headset mike as her fingers played over a greasy keypad, bringing up file after file on the flatscreen behind the desk. 'Look, I don't care what he's doing right now,' she was saying as we walked in, 'but the duty roster says he's the guy in charge of clean-up detail this week.'

Pause. 'Then you wake him up.' She noticed our presence,

nodded once and held up a finger. 'He doesn't know yet? Fine. Tell him the new boss wants him in here with a broom and a trash barrel . . . make it two barrels . . . or he's docked a week's pay, and if I don't see him in fifteen minutes, then the same goes for you. This place is a sty and I didn't make this mess. That's all.'

She pulled the headset down around her neck, sighed deeply, then stood up and looked straight at us. 'Was it as bad as this the last time you were here?' she asked no one in particular.

No one answered for a moment, then Yoshio cleared his throat. 'A little worse, actually,' he said softly. 'Last time we were here, they hadn't taken out the garbage.'

Tillis stared at him, then slowly nodded her head. 'Now it's on the surface. Magnificent.' She stood up from behind the desk and stretched her back. 'Looks like I've got my work cut out for me.'

The Smiths began to murmur vague, embarrassed apologies, but Marianne shook her head. 'Not your fault,' she said flatly. 'The company told me this place was a wreck when they offered me the job. That's why I'm here.' She looked straight at Montrose. 'Captain, I'm sure you and your people don't want to be down here any longer than you have to, but I've found that the records are screwed.'

'How's that?' Saul asked.

She shrugged as she bent over the desk and tapped commands into the keypad. A spreadsheet appeared on the screen behind her; she pointed at the upper right corner of the display, noting the date. 'The last time anyone bothered to update the logbook was two weeks ago. Means we don't have an accurate tally of how much helium-3 we're supposed to be giving you . . . in fact, I suspect the last shipment we were given was probably off by a few hundred tons, since everything I've seen so far looks like guesstimates.'

'Uh-huh.' Montrose rubbed his chin between his fingers. 'You think LeRoy was cooking the books?'

Her eyelids fluttered briefly. 'Maybe. Maybe not. I'll let him take that up with the company when he gets back.' She walked over to the shelf and picked up the litre bottle; the clear liquid sloshed about as she shook it. 'Anyone want a drink? I found the still this came from last night in the galley. Far as I can tell, most everyone down here has been on a bender for the last two months. This was Butt Face's . . . 'cuse me, Mr LeRoy's . . . personal stash.'

She unstopped the bottle and upended it over an overstuffed wastecan, letting the evil-smelling liquor spill over the garbage until she dropped the bottle itself on top of the pile. The new boss smiled briefly. 'The most fun I've had since I've been here was to take an axe to the damn thing. God, you should have heard 'em howl.'

Tillis folded her arms across her chest, looking again at Saul. 'Since B. F. has declined to co-operate, it's up to us to prepare a decent invoice to send to the company. Might take a few hours, but that's the way it is.'

Saul nodded his head. 'I hear you.' He glanced at his watch as he turned toward us. 'I'll meet you guys at . . . ah, let's call it 15.00 ship-time . . . at the main airlock. All right?'

The Smiths nodded their heads, however reluctantly, then slowly filed out of the GM's office. As we edged out of the door and into the rank tunnel, I found Young Bill at my side. 'What are we supposed to do for the next five hours?' I said quietly.

'Keep from getting beat up,' he whispered back.

This was easier said than done.

Yoshio was lucky. He found the base infirmary just down the corridor from the GM's office and went inside to visit with his counterpart on Callisto, a thin young physician named Jesus Caliente. Dr Caliente was one of the few people at Valhalla who had remained sober and reasonably responsible; when we discovered him, Jesus and one of the few AIs that was still functional in the base were unpacking the crates of medical supplies that had been brought down by the *Marius*. Yoshio and I gave him a hand, but when the conversation shifted to bland medical shop-talk that was over my head, I excused myself and went in search of the rest of the *Explorer*'s crew.

I found Leslie, Lynn and Young Bill in the wardroom. The compartment was crowded; at least half the base's complement was in there, and some of their homemade ceramic mugs contained liquor from the still Tillis had destroyed earlier. The new GM might have destroyed the still, but she had yet to ferret out all the bottles in the base.

Lynn was leaning against the far wall, drinking coffee by herself and scowling at everyone who came near. On the other side of the room, Young Bill was in deep conversation with Van Sant, the young woman who had temporarily piloted the *Medici Explorer*. The two of them were talking in subdued tones, looking over their shoulders and sharing quiet laughter at private jokes. They had apparently met before during an earlier trip; this didn't sit well with Lynn, who constantly watched her son, giving him sharp looks which the teenager silently ignored.

Yet there were worse things to be worried about than Young Bill's flirtations. Leslie had hunkered down at a poker table with the four men we had glimpsed earlier. Although she neither contributed nor took anything from the pile of cigarettes in the centre of the table, she was slaughtering them hand after hand, displaying the cool verve of a master cardsharp.

With each hand she won, the temperature at the table rose another degree. Here were four beefy, hard-core spacers who had thought themselves to be the best poker players in the outer solar system, being trounced by a woman who wouldn't even accept the measly stakes on the table. 'Sorry, don't smoke,' Leslie would say, pushing away the hand-rolled cigarettes on the table. 'Let's just do this for fun, OK?'

The four men at the table grumbled and griped, reaching for the bottle on the table, apparently indifferent to the fact that they were ripped while Leslie was stone sober. While Lynn went to the rusting coffee urn to refill her mug, I caught a glimpse of Van Sant whispering in Young Bill's ear. The young man's face coloured slightly; he glanced furtively in his first-mother's direction, but the pilot already had him by the hand and was leading him out the door. When Lynn turned around again, her son was gone. She shot me a look; I shrugged, pretending innocence, and she reluctantly settled back against the wall, casting nervous looks alternately between the door and the card table.

The scenario might have remained tense, but little more, had B. F. LeRoy not walked in. The recently deposed general manager was accompanied by two cronies; all three were ripped to the gills. They slumped down at an adjacent table, each nursing a flask of liquor, and watched Leslie stomp the other poker players for a while until Butt Face belched loudly.

'If she loses the next hand,' he said, 'I wanna see her tits.'

The wardroom fell silent, the overlapping conversation falling away. Leslie's face didn't change. She stared at the four cards in her hand, trying to ignore the surly laughter around her. I glanced at Lynn; she had already put down her mug and was standing erect, her hands on her hips.

Leslie calmly pulled a ten-of-hearts out of her hand and placed it on the table. One of the men sitting across the table from her produced a queen from his hand and slapped it down on top of her card.

'Wanna see her tits?'' LeRoy said more loudly. 'Wanna see what they look like?'

Leslie swallowed hard, then looked up at her partners and managed a nervous grin. 'C'mon, guys,' she said softly. 'Let's keep this friendly.'

They glared at her, unmoved by her appeal. One of them, the man sitting closest to her, barely nodded his head, but the other two were staring at her with dark, baleful eyes. 'You ain't put nothing into the poke,' one of them said, lecherously emphasizing the last word. 'This game's all about risk, y'know?'

The other one's eyes were fastened on her chest. 'Like to see you put a little something on the table,' he said. 'Might make it more interesting.'

'I think it's interesting enough as it is,' Leslie said calmly, studying her hand. At the back of the room, Lynn was touching her jaw with her left hand, murmuring under her breath.

'No, no,' LeRoy muttered, leering openly. 'I wanna see how interesting you can make it.' He held his own hands, palm upwards, near his chest. 'Come down here, you gotta show us yer tits before you play with the boys.'

It wasn't about poker or sex, however much it seemed that way. It was about a roomful of men who had lost control of their lives and wanted to take it out on someone who was easy to harass. Leslie's gender wasn't what had set them off; it was the fact that she had come into their wretched burrow and, by her calm presence alone, had shown them how horrible their lives had become . . . and how they hated her for it.

The prelude to rape was a moment frozen in time: a room gone absolutely quiet, everyone completely still. From somewhere far down the corridor could be heard the sound of running feet, boots pounding against the hard stone floor. A tall, skinny man near the wardroom entrance silently pushed the door shut and stood against it, arms folded across his chest.

Leslie didn't see this, but she sensed the change in attitude. She carefully folded her hands and laid the cards on the table. Eyes downcast, she wordlessly scooted back her chair and stood up as she began to walk away from the table. LeRoy pushed back his own chair and stood up; two of the men who had been sitting at the card table did the same.

'Oh no, you don't,' LeRoy quickly stepped in front of Leslie. 'I'll be damned if I ain't leaving without getting a going-away party.'

Leslie stopped in her tracks, her eyes glancing either way at the men who were beginning to encircle her. Lynn started to move toward her, but suddenly found herself surrounded as well. She tried to push through. Three men grabbed her from behind, two of them wrenching her arms behind her back while the third jammed a dirty cap against her face, cutting off her last shout.

Before I could do anything, I was grabbed from behind by two more men and was hauled back against the wall. I attempted to pull free, and in the next instant I felt the sharp tip of a jackknife against my throat. 'Try it, buddy,' I heard someone say, 'and I'll carve you a new mouth.'

All around us, helium miners were chuckling, whispering to each other. I could hear someone pounding against the door, but the skinny guy who had shut it had put his back against it; like everyone else, he had a scornful, expectant grin on his face.

Leslie's eyes were locked with LeRoy's. 'Don't do this,' she said softly, trying one last time to reason with him. 'If you do . . .'

'Fuck that,' LeRoy said. 'What I do won't matter shit in the long run. This base is mine, sweet thing, and nobody's going to take it from me.' He glanced around at the other men in the rec room. 'Will it, guys?'

Scattered murmurs of assent from those who had surrounded us. Everyone else was too scared to interfere; the innocent were in silent conspiracy with the guilty. Leering at the woman, LeRoy's hands moved to the front of his baggy trousers; there was the slow, ugly sound of his fly being unzipped. 'We can do this easy,' he said, 'or we can do it the . . .

Whatever he was going to say next was lost in the agonized whuff! of his breath leaving his lungs as Leslie kicked her right foot straight up into his groin. He doubled over, his hands clutching at his crotch, but before she could hit him again, the men who had been standing behind Leslie grabbed her and savagely flung her to the floor, pinioning her arms and legs to the filthy carpet with their mass.

Leslie cried out as one of them ripped open the front of her jumpsuit, clawing her skin with his dirty nails. LeRoy painfully straightened up, his eyes seething with murder. 'Fuckin' bitch!' he gasped as he lurched toward her. 'Gonna fuck you till you scream, you lesbo . . . !'

Then the door crashed open as a chair was slammed against it as a battering ram, and the man who had been standing against it was knocked aside as Saul, Young Bill, Yoshio, and Marianne Tillis charged into the room.

The skipper and Yoshio leaped upon the men who were holding Lynn; they were on the floor in a second, taken completely by surprise, with scarcely a couple of punches thrown. Yelling wildly, Young Bill attacked the two men who had pinned Leslie to the floor; before they could make it to their feet, he kicked one straight in the jaw, sending him reeling backward, as the other one scuttled away, holding up his hands as if to protest his innocence.

In the same instant the man who had been restraining me relaxed his grip. I kicked backward blindly, felt the heel of my boot connect with his femur, heard him yell as his arms released me and the knife fell to the floor. Without looking, I shot my right elbow back; another lucky shot caught him straight in the centre of his chest. He gasped and toppled to the floor.

His pal was already backing away. I didn't know why until I heard Marianne Tillis shout: 'Everyone freeze!'

I looked around, saw that she had a small-calibre revolver clutched in both hands. She was aiming at LeRoy. 'Move and you're dead!' she yelled.

Still half-hunched over. LeRoy froze in position as everyone in the room who had not been directly involved in the attempted rape moved back against the walls, trying to melt into the paint. Holding her ripped shirt against her scratched breasts, Leslie began crawling away as Young Bill stepped forward to help her off the floor.

As he did, Marianne's line of fire was blocked for a moment. LeRoy saw his chance. Maybe it was a desperate attempt to regain control, or frustration over a sundered career, or perhaps a last suicidal impulse. Whatever the reason, he howled inchoate rage as he flung himself straight toward the new general manager.

'Down!' Tillis shouted. She didn't wait for Young Bill or Leslie to react; still keeping the gun targeted on LeRoy, she quickly stepped to the left and, in the next instant, squeezed the trigger.

There was a sudden bang! that reverberated off the walls as the .22 bullet hit LeRoy in the right shoulder. He staggered backward; for a second it seemed as if he would drop. Yet, like a wounded bull in blood-rage, he stubbornly lurched forward again, and didn't stop until Tillis fired her pistol again.

Twice again, the rec room was hammered by the sound of gunfire.

The second bullet entered B. F. LeRoy's heart. The third splattered his brains across the floor.

Now there was utter silence in the rec room, save for Leslie softly crying in Young Bill's arms. Everyone else had cleared a wide circle around the *Explorer*'s crew and B. F. LeRoy's corpse. Tillis was still holding the revolver in firing position, heedless of the dark blood that slowly flowed across the floor from the body to the soles of her shoes. The close air held the scent of discharged gunpowder.

'Get your people out of here, Captain,' she murmured over her shoulder to Montrose, never taking her eyes off the men in the room.

Young Bill was already helping Leslie out of the door. As I walked across the room, I noticed that the men around me seemed to have diminished in size. The knife that had been held at my throat had been abandoned on the floor; whoever owned it was too frightened to pick it up. Lynn seemed reluctant to leave; her face was hot with anger, but Yoshio whispered something in her ear that persuaded her to slowly walk out of the room.

Montrose was the last to leave the room. He paused next to Tillis. 'Do you need any . . .?'

'No,' she said coldly, not looking his way. 'You've done enough already, thank you.' She gave him one final glance. 'Now get out of here.'

We were halfway down the corridor when Jamie Van Sant suddenly emerged from behind a half-open hatch. She had heard everything; she went straight to Young Bill and while the rest of the crew hovered nearby the two of them had a short, whispered conversation. He nodded his head; she hugged him tight and held on as the kid looked at Montrose.

'She wants to leave, Captain,' he said quietly. 'If she doesn't go . . .'

Montrose hesitated. His dark eyes flicked back and forth between them. Whatever had occurred between these kids mattered, but not right now; he quickly nodded his head. 'No time to pack,' he said to Jamie. The woman nodded in agreement, still clinging to Bill. 'OK,' he said. 'Let's go.'

We were at the entance hatch, the shore party beginning to climb up the ladder to the EVA dome, when another gunshot rang out from far down the corridor. We stopped and looked around as its echo reverberated off the rock walls of the catacombs . . . then we heard the crash of yet another gunshot, reverberating away into the catacombs.

I looked at Saul. He was staring down the corridor, back toward the rec room. He glanced at me, meeting my questioning gaze with an unpiteous expression.

'Justice,' he whispered.

At least until the bullets run out.

The Weight

OCTOBER 6, 2061: the final day in the Jovian system before the *Medici Explorer* set out for its return to the Moon.

The last hours were spent in preparation for the long journey home. The day before, workers from Valhalla Station had completed the load-in of helium-3 from barges to the three drone freighters. There had been little contact between the Callistians and the crew of the *Explorer*, save for the most perfunctory information exchanged over the comlink. Which was just as well; the Smiths wanted to leave Callisto as soon as possible and put the terrifying incident in the rec room behind them.

Marianna Tillis reached Saul Montrose by radio and apologized profusely for the assault on his people, but offered no explanation for the gunshots we had heard before we had escaped the base, other than to say that the situation was now 'under control'. She told the skipper that a report would be sent to ConSpace and Pax which would fully disclose the circumstances surrounding B. F. LeRoy's death, and assured Montrose that neither he nor his crew would be held responsible for the incident; she did not say, however, whether anyone else had been shot after we had left the scene. Yet she made a point of warning Montrose not to come back down to Valhalla Station, even when the captain asked if she wanted to send LeRoy's body back to earth aboard the explorer.

'We have our own graveyard, Captain,' she said. 'He'll be buried there. Besides, you and your crew may not be very welcome down here right now.

'And the next mission?' Montrose asked.

'I'll leave that up to the Smiths' good sense,' Tillis replied.

To which Geoff Smith-Makepeace, usually the least opinionated of the family, later offered a shorthand response that spoke for the feelings of the entire family: 'When hell freezes over.' Which was a fairly accurate description of Callisto itself.

Two of Valhalla's former station members, Casey Nimersheim and Jamie Van Sant, were only too glad to be going home, even though it meant that their contracts were being prematurely terminated. Before they were put into biostasis for the trip home, the women told Leslie that what had happened to her was not uncommon in Valhalla; while on Callisto, both of them had been subjected to rape attempts by male crewmen, each escaping by only luck or happenstance. Leslie was not comforted by their stories; she swore to them that, once radio contact with Earth was possible, she would immediately file a report of her own and would demand that ConSpace send security personnel to Callisto to make sure that nothing like this happened again.

Montrose agreed to second Leslie's report, but warned her that ConSpace's directors might not take immediate action. 'The company's primary interest is in keeping the pipeline open, Les,' he said, not unkindly. 'So long as they get what they want, the directors really don't care what happens to the people who work out here.'

'Fuck you, sir,' Leslie said before she stormed off the bridge.

And then there was the mystery of Jamie Van Sant herself. After all, she and Young Bill had disappeared from the rec room not long before the assault had taken place, and although Young Bill later admitted to the captain that the two of them had gone to her quarters, he insisted that 'nothing' had happened. And, as Saul pointed out after he had received her records from Valhalla Station, Van Sant was almost eight years older than Young Bill; she was an adult while he was still a man-child. An infatuation maybe, but full-scale romance? Unlikely.

Over the next couple of days before Yoshio sealed Jamie in a zombie tank, though, the two young people were nearly insepar-able . . . and once, when Betsy was visiting the wardroom for a quick snack before reporting to duty, she discovered them in what she later described as 'a true meeting of the minds', although she refused to go into details.

Were they or weren't they? Old Bill and Lynn had better sense than to stick their noses where they didn't belong, and although Saul grinned whenever the subject came up at the mess table and

Young Bill was subjected to relentless teasing by Wendy and Kaneko, never once did the kid break silence. He grinned sheepishly and turned red when Geoff or Leslie made discreet inquiries, or glowered and stalked off when Uncle Yoshio tried to give him an obligatory lecture on sexual hygiene, but throughout he kept his own counsel.

The morning of the launch, when Yoshio put Jamie into biostasis, Young Bill escorted her down to the hibernation deck. He held her hand as Yoshio administered the drugs which would put her into an artificial coma, then stood beside the zombie tank until she was sound asleep, leaving only after his first-father summoned him by comlink for EVA duty.

I was standing next to the hibernation bay hatch, waiting for Yoshio to give me a final physical, so I watched this scene as it took place. I was scheduled to be put into my own tank shortly after the *Medici Explorer* left Jupiter. When Young Bill finally turned away from Jamie's tank and walked out of the bay, he paused at the hatchway.

'She's going to Scotland with me,' he whispered, a loopy, lovesick grin spread across his face.

I smiled back at him and slapped him on the shoulder. The teenager exited the compartment, heading up the Arm toward the main airlock. Yoshio had me seated on an examination table and was breaking out his instruments when I heard a war-whoop from the access shaft.

Yoshio raised an eyebrow. I tried to contain my smile. Neither of us dreamed that this was the last time either of us would see Young Bill alive.

In space, death is quick and merciless. It often comes without warning; even the simplest mistake can snuff out a life in the time it takes for you to read these words. A thousand things can go wrong, and all it takes is a moment of carelessness. The hubris of the soul is no match for the relentless nature of the cosmos.

One of the *Explorer*'s manoeuvring engines had developed problems during the outbound leg of the voyage. In hindsight, I remembered that Saul had mentioned this to me after I had been revived from biostasis five days earlier. The engine wasn't gimball-ing correctly; a secondary servomotor kept freezing up. Old Bill had corrected the glitch once before, but during pre-launch checkout he and Saul found that the problem had reappeared.

Normally, this was something an AI would have been sent to fix, yet because Tiger had been left on Amalthea and none of the other robots were designed for this sort of labour, it meant that a crewmember had to do the dirty work. Old Bill couldn't do the job, though; his over-exposure to radiation during the rescue mission had confined him to the interior of the vessel. This meant that Young Bill had to go EVA.

He went out in the ship's service bug, a tiny gumdrop-shaped vehicle with double-jointed RWS arms, used for in-flight repair missions. Bill had been thoroughly trained and checked out for the bug; indeed, this was the third time he had piloted the vehicle during a flight. While Betsy, his dad and Saul monitored from the bridge, he took the bug out from its socket on the hub, jetted around the ship's rotating arms, and gently manoeuvred the little one-person craft until he reached the manoeuvring engines behind the radiation shield.

The repair operation took less than an hour. A thermocouple had come loose again, just as his first-father suspected; following his instructions, Young Bill replaced it with a new unit. Saul and Old Bill ran a systems-test, bringing the engine to pre-ignition status. The replacement held up, and Old Bill told his son to come home.

Later, after the accident, I listened to the flight-recorder tape.

Old Bill: *'OK, that's it . . . come on home. Over.'*

Young Bill: *'Right. Be there in a minute. Over.'*

There was a brief pause, lasting a couple of minutes as the kid uncoupled the bug's magnetic grapple from the fuselage, then: *'Hey, I wanna try something neat . . .'*

Saul: *'What's that? Over.'*

Young Bill: *'Wait. Watch the screen. You'll see. Over.'*

Old Bill: *'Bill, don't go messing around out there . .'*

Young Bill: *'Don't worry. You'll love it. It's a surprise. Over.'*

By now the bug had cleared the engine array and the shield. Young Bill should have taken the bug back the way he came, past the fuel tanks and around the rotating arms until he reached the hub. Everyone on the bridge was watching what he was doing . . . right up until the moment he impulsively decided to take a shortcut.

Young Bill: '*Here we go. Straight through the arms.*'

Saul: '*Bill, don't do it!*'

A half-second lapsed as the bug's engine flared and the little vehicle raced for a momentary gap between the rotating arms. It was making a dash between the twirling vanes of a windmill; it could be done, if your timing was correct. Had Bill's calculations been a little more certain, his wild stunt would have been just that, a reckless wager between himself and fate.

He lost the bet.

Arm Two slammed into the bug at two RPMs, squashing the tiny vehicle like a chestnut beneath a jackhammer. On the tape, his last scream was cut short by the implosion of the bug's fuselage, and both noises are all but lost beneath the sound of his father's anguished howl.

In two seconds, Young Bill was dead.

In the end, there was a shrouded corpse, sealed inside an airtight bag and wrapped within layers of white plastic and reflective silver foil, strapped to the outer hull of Arm One. It was not the first time the *Medici Explorer* returned from space with a body bag on its fuselage, but it was the saddest occasion; this time, the body was that of one of its own crewmembers.

William Smith-Tate, Jr would not make his last voyage back to the Moon alone. Marlon Bellafonte's body had already been tied to the outside of Arm One. There was simply no way they could be kept within the vessel for the duration of the return voyage, and – contrary to the cliché fostered by dozens of films and novels – bodies of deceased spacers were not commonly jettisoned from airlocks. There would be no 'burial in space' for Young Bill or Bellafonte, nor would they occupy graves in the harsh rocky ground of Callisto. From distant Earth they had come, and to the earth they would return.

Captain Montrose and Yoshio Smith-Tanaka were the only crewmembers who were up to the grim chore; everyone else was in shock. They watched from the bridge as the two men, wearing hardsuits and magnetic overshoes, removed the shrouded corpse from the main airlock and gently hauled it to the Arm, whose rotation had been stopped after the accident.

Save for the everpresent background sound of purring, chittering electronics, the compartment was silent as the body was lashed to the arm with nylon cords. Even the comlink had been turned down low so that Saul's and Yoshio's voices were only a faint whisper. Geoff gazed at the screen, his hands folded together in his lap, seemingly emotionless except for the trembling of his lower lip. Betsy's face was turned away, watching the orbital patterns on her console's holos; every now and then she raised a hand to dawb away the tears which seeped from her eyes. Leslie held Wendy and Kaneko in her arms, trying to console the crying children even though she herself was on the verge of breaking down.

As for William and Lynn Smith-Tate, they stood apart from the others near the back of the compartment, stolidly watching as their son was tied to the outer hull of the vessel. Lynn was groggy from the sedatives Yoshio had administered to her after the accident, yet she clung to her first-husband's shoulder, occasionally murmuring something under her breath, while Old Bill stared stolidly at the screen, never saying a word, his face rarely showing any emotion. His left hand was on his first-wife's shoulder; tucked beneath his right arm was a leatherbound copy of *The Book of Mormon*.

When Saul and Yoshio were finished, they stepped back from Young Bill, walking slowly across the hull on the magnetic soles of their boots. They said nothing, but Old Bill didn't need a cue. He opened the holy book and, in an unnaturally soft and trembling voice, began to read from Alma, Chapter 40, Verses 11 and 12:

' "Now, concerning the state of the soul between death and the resurrection – Behold, it has been made known unto me by an angel, that the spirits of all men, as soon as they are departed from this mortal body, yea, the spirits of all men, whether they be good or evil, are taken home to that God who gave them life." '

He paused, swallowed hard, and went on. ' "And then shall it come to pass that the spirits of those who are righteous are received into a state of happiness, which is called paradise, a state of rest, a state of peace, where they shall rest from all their troubles and from all care, and sorrow." '

He closed the book, shut his eyes and lowered his head. 'In the name of Jesus Christ, Amen.'

All of us did the same. Young Bill's funeral was still many months away. For the time being, this was the best any of us could do.

'*Amen.*' Saul said at last over the comlink. His voice was hoarse. '*Let's secure for launch and get the . . . let's get out of this place.*'

When I opened my eyes and raised my head again, the first thing I happened to see was the open hatch of the observation blister where Young Bill had spent so much of his time. The wingback chair within the tiny sphere was empty, the telescope eyepiece untouched since when he had last used it.

As the Smiths quietly went to work, preparing the imminent departure of the *Medici Explorer* from Callisto, for the first time since his death, I felt the sting of tears at the corners of my eyes.

Two hours later, the *Medici Explorer* fired its main engines and began the long trip back to the inner solar system. Behind it followed its three freighters, each fully laden with helium-3; on the bridge screens, we could see the convoy as it moved out of parking orbit above Callisto, their engine-thrusts appearing as bright pinpricks against the black sky.

The mission had been completed. We were going home. There was no sense of accomplishment, though, only a hollow sensation in the guts of everyone aboard the vessel. The launch was carried out in a subdued manner, Saul listlessly murmuring the countdown to primary ignition, the rest of the crew performing their duties as if they were only going through the motions. The bridge was much more quiet this time. No one yelled with teenage excitement as we left Jupiter behind and began our long march through space.

Shortly after launch, once all stations had been secured and everything had been put on automatic, the Smiths quietly excused themselves from duty and went below to the wardroom. What they said or did down there, though, I do not know, for neither the skipper nor I were invited to join them. Saul and I understood; it was time for the family to come together and share their grief in private.

We remained on the bridge instead, standing third watch. Indeed, it would be my last watch on the *Medici Explorer*; in a few hours, I was scheduled to go down to the hibernation deck myself, where Yoshio would help me into a zombie tank and inject me with drugs that would put me in suspended animation for the duration of the voyage. We sat together in the command centre the captain and I, sipping coffee, quietly watching the screens as Jupiter and its moons gradually receded behind us. There seemed to be little left for either of us to say to one another. Young Bill was gone; a hole had been punched in each of our hearts.

After a time, though, the Captain unbuckled his seat belt and rose from his chair. 'Watch the deck for a moment, will you?' he said. 'I'll be back in a minute.'

I nodded, expecting him to go visit the head, but instead he pushed himself over to the access hatch. In another moment he was through the hatch and down the ladder, leaving the command centre in my care.

I was now alone in the bridge, for the first time since I had begun the long journey to Jupiter. All around me were holoscreens and TV monitors, randomly blinking lights and whispering instruments. The ship was alive, yet at the same time it was dead, as empty as the chairs around me.

For the moment, I was the captain of the *Medici Explorer*.

I stood up and slowly walked around the bridge, stopping at every duty station, touching the back of each chair. Here was where Betsy sat; here was Geoff's post. This was where Leslie monitored the life-support systems, and Old Bill sat here at the engineering console. Their places were vacant now, but the vessel seemed to function perfectly in their absence . . .

Maybe it was a little too much to ask of humans to go out here, out to the cold depths of space where life was so fragile and madness lurked beneath the crusts of desolate worlds. Perhaps robots could do this hard job just as easily, if not better. No one mourned when Tiger was sacrificed on Amalthea; an AI has no family, no friends, no one to miss it except for the slight inconvenience its sudden absence posed. It could be replaced.

People aren't like that.

So why are we out here?

I was still standing in the centre of the bridge, looking at nothing in particular, thinking about all I had witnessed, when I heard Saul climb up the ladder and re-enter the compartment. Lost in reflection, I didn't look around until he tapped my shoulder.

'He would have wanted you to have this,' he said softly as I turned around, then he placed something in my hand: Young Bill's tennis ball, taken from his hiding-place in the storage locker where I had discovered him playing handball.

I gazed at the frayed yellow ball, imagining that I could still hear the relentless bounce it made against the walls and ceiling of the compartment. 'You knew it was there?' I asked.

He nodded his head. 'Yeah, I knew about it. Like I knew you would find him down there when I sent you to look for him.' He paused. 'He liked you, Elliot. He had a family and a captain, but for a little while there he had you for a friend. I'm glad you were here for him.'

Even as I write these words, with the events I have described millions of miles distant and nearly a year in the past, the ball is on a shelf above my desk. I have looked up at it often as I've composed this chronicle. Sometimes I take it down from the shelf and bounce it off the wall of my office. Yet that wasn't Young Bill's final gift.

'Come here,' Saul said. 'You need to see this.'

He took me to the observation blister where Bill had often sat, helped me into the bubble and strapped me into the chair, adjusted the periscope-like mount and showed me how to work the telescope. When I was ready, he backed out of the little sphere and sealed the hatch; I settled back in the wingbacked chair, pulled the binocular eyepiece against my face, and touched the stud that opened the shutter.

Here again was Jupiter, looming large against infinite space, a king surrounded by his royal court. Fiery Io and icy Callisto, pale blue Europa and multicoloured Ganymede, and all the lesser worlds: Leda, Himalia, Elara, Lysithea, Anake, Carme, Pasiphae, Sinope . . . and tiny Amalthea. As different as members of a family, each as remote from the other yet bonded by common bonds of gravity and shared heritage.

I gazed upon them as the *Medici Explorer* fell toward the sun, bearing the weight of our dreams.